Fifteen Minutes

by Amanda Prowse

Lionhead Media Publishing

Table of Contents

Praise for Amanda Prowse

Dedication

Also by Amanda Prowse

Chapter One - Chen

Chapter Two - Violet Katherine Drummond

Chapter Three - Lewis Mark Noble

Chapter Four - Ruby Jade Brown

Chapter Five - Verity Louise Clarke

Chapter Six - Benjamin Stokes-Rattigan

Chapter Seven - Mikey Charles Frewin

Epilogue - Chen

About The Author - Amanda Prowse

Praise for Amanda Prowse

'Amanda Prowse is "The Queen of Family Drama"' –
Daily Mail

'You'll fall in love with this...' –
Cosmopolitan

'Powerful and emotional drama that packs a real punch' –
Heat

'Heartbreaking and heartwarming in equal measure' –
The Lady

'Deeply moving and emotional' –
Red

'Handles her explosive subjects with delicate skill' –
Daily Mail

'Captivating, heartbreaking and superbly written' –
Closer

'Uplifting and positive but you will still need a box of tissues' – Hello!

ISBN 978-1-915-400-09-3 (paperback)

ASIN B0GP9FWP5K *(eBook)*

FIRST EDITION

Cover design by Lionhead Media Publishing

Dedication

This is a fanciful story no doubt.

And one I dedicate to every single person who has lost someone they love.

When grief hits me hard, often at the most unexpected of moments, and I miss them with a pain that is visceral, I imagine what it might be like to have fifteen minutes with them.

To tell them one more time that I love them, to share news of our family and to remind myself of the small details about them that have started to fade.

It's an idea that brings me great comfort, the thought that I might see them just once more, for fifteen minutes.

Now, wouldn't that be something…

Also by Amanda Prowse

NOVELS

Poppy Day

What Have I Done

Clover's Child

A Little Love

Will You Remember Me?

Christmas for One

A Mother's Story

Perfect Daughter

The Second Chance Café (was 'The Christmas Café')

Three and a Half Heartbeats

Another Love

My Husband's Wife

I Won't be Home for Christmas

The Food of Love

The Idea of You

The Art of Hiding

Anna

Theo

Kitty (was 'How to Fall in Love Again; Kitty's Story')

The Coordinates of Loss

The Girl in the Corner

The Things I Know

The Light in the Hallway

The Day She Came Back.

An Ordinary Life

Waiting to Begin

To Love and Be Loved

Picking Up the Pieces

All Good Things

Swimming to Lundy

This One Life

Ever After

Life as Planned

The Way Home (publishing August 2026)

Holding On Tight (publishing January 2027)

MEMOIRS

The Boy Between

Women Like Us

NOVELLAS

The Game

Something Quite Beautiful

A Christmas Wish

The Ten Pound Ticket

Imogen's Baby

Miss Potterton's Birthday Tea

Mr Portobello's Morning Paper

I Wish...

A Whole Heap of Wishes

A Wish for Forgiveness

Fifteen Minutes

COLLECTION OF THE FIRST SEVEN NOVELLAS

Stories from the Heart

Chapter One - Chen

Do you ever think about time? Who conceived it, made the rules, set the boundaries?

I know I do.

I think of little else!

Can you imagine a life without the clocks, watches, sundials, hourglasses, chimes, alarms, buzzers and countdowns that run our lives?

The idea of just being. Eating when hungry. Sleeping when tired. Curling up in the dark. Stretching in the sun. Working when you have the inclination.

Oh, what freedom. What simplicity.

Yet quite impossible. I should know.

We all understand it, don't we? The concept of time.

How long will that take?

When will it arrive?

What time can I expect you?

You're late!

It ends at...

You just missed it...

Too early.

When?

The past, present and future, rolling on and on ad infinitum as we watch the hands of the clock sweep round and around, eating up our lives until it spins faster and faster and all we can do is hold our breath and jump in. Lost to our very own ending.

Indeed, it's how we measure our life on Earth: time of birth, time of death.

Two days plucked by the Universe, made important to you and yours alone, as granite stones and listing wooden crosses set in soil the world over will attest. Small numbers etched in memoriam with a dash between the two. Think about it, some would argue that dash is the most important piece of information, indicating the amount of time we were gifted in a life that nearly always feels infinite, until it's not.

That carved notch the overriding summary of your existence from which strangers will decide whether you were *taken too soon* or had *a really good innings*. It seems important, how long you endured, ran your race, despite, in nearly all cases, your lack of ability to influence such a thing.

I myself don't fully understand the importance placed on longevity, having, in my time, known short lives that had the most extraordinary impact! And some of the longest that have been nothing but dull, lonely and lacking in effect or achievement.

To be clear, by impact I mean not the climbing of mountains, the attainment of wealth or any imagined heroics, but more the everyday kindness that means the person in question made a difference to *someone.*

I believe this is the real magic – a smiling face, a kind word, an arm of support, a nod of encouragement – these, my friend, are the levers of change! How I wish more of us employed them. Now what a world that would be.

Yet here we are, bound by the ticking clock, as our hearts beat out its rhythm, and our feet march to its tune.

Yet did you know that time does not actually exist? That's right. The very first time-makers used the sun and the moon as markers. There was the waking time, the sleeping time, the dark time, the light time – you get the gist.

In our quest to make sense of our world, to grasp at something tangible in the dark confusion of existence, we allow our whole lives – and every task within it – to be marked by units of time. We are beholden to it, we can't cheat it, avoid it or hide from it. We can't make it go faster or slower, no matter how much we might wish. And when our time is up – we simply cease to be. Right?

Wrong!

So wrong.

What if I told you that time was not as unyielding as you might believe? What if I told you it was in fact a fluid, bendable thing and that there are gaps in it, if you know where to look?

I know, curious, isn't it?

Like someone asking you for the first time to picture what lies beyond our known Universe – POW! I know my childhood brain stuttered and I felt entirely flummoxed by the question, thrown by the possibilities and absolutely shaken that it had not occurred to me to think of it earlier.

I expect you're wondering who I am?

That's a good question.

I'm always the person you would least suspect.

My name is Chen. I am a master of time.

One of many, I might add. Although, if it isn't too presumptuous of me to say, I am one of the best. I don't doubt that any of us born for such an art can easily understand and execute the mechanics of the job. My specialism, I believe, and what sets me apart, is understanding how it affects humankind, the emotional response, the long-lasting effect of my role. I choose my recipients wisely and with an innate ability to select only the most deserving. A skill no less. But enough about me. You shall see my work for itself as these pages unfold. And please ask yourself, did I choose wisely?

I do hope so.

Maybe you think yourself an ideal candidate for such a gift?

Well, we can talk about that.

So, how is time fluid? I shan't bore you with the physics, won't pretend that even I fully understand the quirk that allows for the manipulation of this most fundamental thing. But what if I told you that the creators of time made a small error, an oversight if you will. Has this got your interest? It should. You want to know how? You want to know when this error occurs? Come closer and I shall whisper:

Every single second of every day.

Now to explain it in a way that keeps it simple.

How about this – imagine you're a bank. A bank with a million accounts and each account has billions and billions of dollars in it. Interest on these accounts fluctuates somewhat – meaning the balance rises and falls. Does that money really exist? Or is it no more than a number on a screen? I guess it only exists when it comes to cashing in. When someone with a big old leather holdall dumps it on the counter and asks for their billions of dollars to take away.

And whilst it might be easy to press a button, call up the balance and arrange for the cash to be deposited in fat bundles of dough, the nickels and dimes that make the interest, the small 0.00000000000000000000000000000001 figure that lurks irritatingly on the bottom line in the echo chamber of fiscal holdings? Well, this little guy, he gets missed; he gets lost.

Big deal! I hear you say, and you're right.

That 0.00000000000000000000000000000001 is no big deal.

Not when the account you're emptying has billions of big ones in it! Easier to ignore him, to let him stay quietly nestled, hidden, behind those fat rolls of cash.

But what if the number of accounts where this tiny amount lurks are themselves in the billion? What then? Well then, my friend, it becomes a big deal, a very big deal.

It amounts to something.

This, crudely, and in short, is what happens with time.

In the simplest of terms, what I am talking about are the minutes between the hours. The seconds between the minutes. The milliseconds between the seconds and stitching them together to provide a patch that I, and others like me, can put to good use.

Time that's unaccounted for, if you will, unallocated. Like the very smallest denomination of currency that people don't want rattling around in their pocket and leave in a change dish on a grubby countertop. It's the same. To gather all those tiny coins would make a handsome sum if gathered the world over – can you *imagine?*

These miniscule fragments of time are of no real interest to anyone apart from maybe those with legal requirement of a data stamp on a transaction, deposition or alibi. Or those with a healthy bet on a nag or any other race where the placing of a nose, arm, foot, hoof or wheel means the difference between going home with a swagger and a tale of winning or heading for the doghouse with a rumble in your empty stomach and a hole in your shoe and pocket.

Yes, those spaces between milliseconds – when ignored – become valuable. I, we, gather them up and string them together, all these little gaps since the dawn of time, enabling us to claw back hours and hours and hours. And that's precisely what we do.

We bunch them together and when we have enough – roughly twice or three times every few years, give or take – we offer them back, hand them out.

Who do we hand them out to? Anyone who has been nominated, anyone we select.

I mean, not indiscriminately; we don't just scatter them around for folk to pick up – lying like russet leaves on the pavement after a fall wind, can you imagine? No, we choose wisely.

I choose wisely.

Anyone can make a nomination, a plea – as long as they make it in the right place and in the right way – but that's probably not something you want to think about. Or need to worry about.

Make no mistake, this gift I bring doesn't come without certain rules and doesn't come without consequences. Because here's the biggie – we can give you *any* fifteen minutes. *Any* fifteen minutes of your life that you'd like to revisit. As long as it's spent with someone who is no longer with you.

Did I mention that? It's about a glimpse, a chance to right a wrong, ask that burning question or maybe just be held, one last time. To have that final conversation or steal a kiss from the one you miss the most, the one with whom you have unfinished business.

Wonderful, right?

Think about it – when or, more specifically, who in your life would you choose?

It just so happens that I am about to make my approaches to the lucky recipients.

Wanna tag along? I don't mind if you do.

But, please, do remember to keep one eye on the clock.

Chapter Two - Violet Katherine Drummond

Aged 98

Vauxhall, London

'Which would you prefer, Nan?' Natalie held up the two cartons, which, to Violet's milky old eyes, looked exactly the same.

'What's the difference?' she squinted, none the wiser.

'One's got bits in it and the other no bits,' her granddaughter explained with the distinct undertone of impatience, as she lifted first one carton then the next.

'Oh, no bits. Thank you.'

Natalie put the orange juice with bits back in the fridge and the other into the shopping trolley that was fixed to the front of Violet's wheelchair – a nifty invention that certainly made supermarket trips a bit easier.

'D'you need ham? I know you like a bit of ham on Boxing Day.'

'No, dear. I'm not eating much. Wouldn't get through a whole packet of ham, it'd be a waste. I hate waste.'

She ate like a little bird. In fact, there were entire days when all the sustenance she required was a cup or two of tea and a reluctant bite of a banana with which to swallow her plethora of glossy little pills that came in an array of vibrant colours.

'Do you need loo roll, Nan?'

'Probably.' She certainly got through enough of the stuff.

Even the questions as they trundled the strip lit aisles were banal and irritating. She knew why Natalie insisted on loading her into the car, folding her wheelchair into the back and pushing her around the supermarket, even though her granddaughter could easily pick up the few things she needed. She did it to keep Violet moving, keep her mind active and to get her out into the real world where real people lurked. It seemed to take on extra importance at this time of year, aware as they all were that this might well be her last Christmas. Violet wasn't stupid, and knew they'd been thinking and pondering this very thing for at least the last decade.

Yet here they were.

She was thankful, of course she was, to be so attended to, but also, at some level, wished Natalie would leave her be in the warm chair by the window. Let her stay home to listen to the radio, sip tea, and chit-chat to Darling. *Darling!* This the name of her carer who came in each day and treated her like she was made of glass, a thing so precious. Her little voice was sweet, her frame tiny. It had been a revelation to learn that Darling was actually made of steel. She'd arrived from the Philippines eighteen months ago with no more than a small bag of clothes and the address of a cousin's cousin, written on a scrap of paper. Violet knew it took mettle to make a move so bold, to be so brave, and she loved her for it.

This weekly trawl around the supermarket, which felt more like a performance than a necessity, always ended in the café inside the superstore, where she and Natalie sipped weak, tepid tea and shared a sticky bun, which her granddaughter always cut into three pieces. Two for her and one for Violet. Today was no exception. The café was bedecked in baubles and thin tinsel. The wan-faced staff wore moronic elf hats and striped tights. She couldn't imagine being asked to wear such things in her working life. Not that it would have been fitting for the secretary of the chairman.

What she'd never say, never would and never could, was that coming out into the real world like this was, in fact, a horrible thing for her. A reminder that she was now no more than an observer, a trick of the light, on the edge of society – waiting to go, be called, keel over, stop. Whatever you wanted to call it. Yet death, it seemed, took joy in making her wait. Well-meaning visitors and family alike told her that a long life was a blessing. She'd smile, nod and fold her knobbly knuckled hands into her narrow lap and silently agree. It was easier than leaning forward with fire in her eyes and raging that it was no such thing! No gift! No blessing! Sitting each day, in discomfort and pain, as the hours limped on monotonously, punctuated only by trips to the bathroom or a visit from an inquisitive robin who might linger on the windowsill.

Old age was a punishment that she had no choice other than to accept graciously, to endure. And here she now sat doing her best to tune out the piped carols that filled the room, to not wince at the shrill call of excited toddlers at play and ignore the stench of fried food that floated in the air and clung to the wipe clean surfaces, while she and Natalie shared a sticky bun. Her granddaughter glanced repeatedly at the clock on her phone which made Violet feel miserable, vulnerable, and burdensome all at the same time.

'Just popping out to call André.'

Natalie left the table and Violet felt her shoulders relax a little, while simultaneously envying the girl the fresh air that awaited while she purred down the phone and fawned over the weasel-faced loser who treated her like dirt. Natalie's questions and chatter when she spoke to him, underpinned with a needy whine that was as unbecoming as it was desperate. It saddened Violet to hear. Not that there was any point in stating this or raising a concern. Hadn't been much point in sharing an opinion on anything since she'd hit her eighties when it felt like she was humoured and tolerated rather than paid heed to. As if all her experience counted for nothing. So she listened, one ear cocked, to tales of woe or joy, conversations between her high-pitched daughters and their daughters who all seemed to think they invented love, sex, heartache, and loss.

The idiots.

Violet huffed, what did they know about loss? These kids who hadn't lived at the beck and call of a siren, as bricks, burning timbers and life as they knew it fell all around them. Lives and homes turned to ash in less time than you'd think. She heard that siren still in the early hours, woke from sleep to the imagined sound, the acrid smell of smoke still in her nostrils. It had been nothing short of petrifying, hell on earth. During the chaos, among the mayhem, she would mentally reach out, calling silently, to a man who was not hers, *come home to me, come safely home to me my love…*

'Excuse me?'

Violet looked up at the man who smiled and pointed at the seat her granddaughter had only just vacated.

'Yes?' She gripped her handbag. Wary of getting her purse nicked and losing the fourteen pounds and eighty-three pence that lurked inside it. Not naturally mistrustful, but the many headlines and whispered gossip at the hair salon encouraged her to get better at it, to doubt the intentions of strangers and to be on guard, just in case.

'Is this seat taken?'

'Well, my granddaughter was sitting there, but now she's—'

'That's okay, I won't be long.' He sat down, and Violet looked over his shoulder, willing Natalie to come back. She didn't like sitting so close to the man.

'It's Violet, isn't it?'

'Do I know you?'

A little forgetful, she was now embarrassed that this man might be known to her, someone who had slipped through the ever-widening net of her memory, until all that remained were the biggest and most impactful moments, memories, and people. She stared at his padded gilet, a clue, no doubt, but no, she couldn't place his smiling face. A nice face, actually. His eyes bright, expression open, skin smooth, mouth kind.

'In a manner, yes. I need to speak quickly, as what I have to say is of the utmost importance and we don't have long.'

'I'm not buying anything, if that's what you're after. And I only give to my favourite charities—'

'Violet,' he said her name again, interrupting her. Now she saw the urgency in the intensity of his stare. She stopped talking. 'My name is Chen.'

'Hello.'

'Hello,' he smiled widely. 'Sometimes we have the luxury to talk at length, to explain, but not today, and so I must calmly, yet expeditiously, get to the point.'

‘I wish you would!’ she spoke only half in jest.

‘What I’m about to tell you will sound strange, unbelievable but, it’s important you understand that I will not and never have told a lie.’

‘If you say so!’ She wished Natalie would hurry; this man was giving her strong nutcase vibes.

‘What would you say if I told you that you could spend time with someone you have lost, someone who has died. What if I said you got to see them again?’

‘I’d say you were a loon and I’d ask the next person who walks past to undo my brake and I’d wheel myself off to wherever you were not!’ she spoke plainly. ‘I don’t believe in mediums or any of that hokum! And I don’t want to hear it if you have a message from Jesus, thank you very much!’ It angered her. She might be old, frail even, but the fact he thought he could take advantage of her in this way was galling.

‘I get that a lot,’ he remained unflustered. ‘but again I promise you that I have never and will never tell you a lie.’ He leaned forward on the tabletop and spoke with urgency. ‘This Saturday, in the hour before midnight, you have the chance to spend fifteen minutes with someone who has gone before you. All you have to do is stay in your chair, close your eyes and, when you open them, it will be a repeat of the time you have chosen to live again with them when they were alive, just as it was.’

‘Is that right?’ She craned her neck towards the door. Where the hell was Natalie?

‘There are some rules, very important rules, Violet. You can’t leave the room, or you will find yourself back home. You mustn’t tell the person you are with that they have died or give them any information that you think might prevent their death. It would make no difference.’

‘I’d like you to stop talking to me, you loon box!’

Chen carried on as if she hadn’t spoken.

‘You cannot change history, can’t undo the thing that has been done, but that kind of disclosure can have the most distressing and disastrous effect on them at a time when they are ailing, oblivious or at peace. It would be cruel, the cruellest. Also they cannot know that they are only there for fifteen minutes. If you breach any of these conditions, they will disappear immediately, and you will lose all that remains of your time.’

‘Why are you saying this to me? Bugger off! Please go away! I want you to leave me alone!’ She felt the uncomfortable rise of emotion in her throat; his jest was cruel and unnecessary.

‘Who will you pick, Violet? Harry?’

To hear her husband’s name on his lips was jarring and emotional. Sixteen years gone, and how she yearned for him! Missing him as much today as she had on that first day, knowing without him her life was subdued, diluted, and her potential for joy so diminished it made waking each morning to face a day on the planet without him harder than she could possibly have imagined.

It was trickery – of that there was no doubt – but the man was extremely convincing. Her heart raced.

'Or David' he asked.

'Da…' she felt her mouth fall open. To hear his name, the little boy who had been born too soon, fighting for the brief time he lay in her arms, a name she hadn't shared with anyone, ever. 'How?'

'Or your mother, Dinah?'

'Who are you?' Her voice now no more than a whisper, she placed her trembling hand over her mouth.

'I'm Chen. I'll leave you now, Violet. Choose wisely and know that it's a wonderful thing to be given this chance, a really wonderful thing.'

He stood as Natalie walked briskly towards the table, her expression close to tears, suggesting the call with weasel face hadn't gone too well.

'Happy Christmas, Violet.'

'Hap, happy Christmas,' she managed, watching as he walked away, lifting his hand in a small wave as Natalie passed him by.

'Who the bloody hell was that?' Her granddaughter reached for a chunk of bun and pushed it into her mouth.

'That was Chen.' Violet fished up her sleeve for her handkerchief and blew her nose. It was fanciful, trickery, ridiculous, and yet a thought so glorious she allowed herself to be quite taken by the absurdity of it all.

The question was, if it *were* possible, who would she choose?

***

Chen's words occupied her thoughts, making her a distracted guest when she was wheeled to her daughter's house and placed in front of the TV while the family chattered their plans, grew tipsy on bubbly wine, wrapped gifts and gorged on chocolates that came in a plastic tub that back in her day had been a useful metal tin. The family took it in turns to walk over to where she had been plonked and squeeze her shoulder, smiling into her face like she was a baby,

'You all right?'

This before offering her another cup of tea. It was bewildering to her; how much liquid did they think she needed?

Safely home, Violet was aware it was Saturday. A day that had loomed in her thoughts since meeting Chen. Trying not to give any heed to his absurd proposal, yet still with a tingle of excitement in her veins, quite taken with the idea. Like having a lottery ticket tucked into your pocket and dreaming of what you might do with the unlikely win.

Darling had settled her for the evening and adhered to Violet's request to be left in her chair. It was one of the loveliest things about her carer, the fact she didn't try and explain what might be best or speak overly loudly or slowly as if Violet was a dum-dum. Instead, she simply nodded, 'Sure.' And did as Violet asked, whatever she asked. Giving equity to their interactions – despite the nature of their association – which meant more than Violet could ever express.

Sitting in the chair, with the usual hum of pain in her hips and throb of discomfort in her knees, she listened as the night fell quiet. There was a stillness in the air, the sky was clear, allowing for the majesty of stars to shine brightly in the inky blue canopy. The kind of night when magic felt possible!

'You're a silly old fool is what you are.'

Violet chuckled, as she settled back and closed her eyes, waiting for the clock to strike and knowing that she would feel like a proper dunce when she opened them again and found it all to be a ruse. A silly, preposterous distraction when she was old enough to know better.

Unsure how long she sat quietly, Violet had the strangest feeling, as if she were sinking, and the chair shifted beneath her. There was a sensation of floating, so much so that she held onto the arms to stop herself from falling.

It wasn't that she was sinking, not at all, but rather that her tiny frame seemed to lift in the seat as if, without the weight of age and the wearying experience of life dragging down her bones, she was a feather! Nimble! Tiny!

Still with her eyes closed, she was struck by a smell, so evocative it took her breath away. It was the unmistakable scent of her parents' home. A smell she didn't know she had forgotten. A combination of cooked vegetables, the slightly sour odour of washing that was nearly dry yet not rigorously clean, the beeswax polish used to buff the sideboards and the lavender water her mother liked to douse herself in post bath. A unique blend, a heady bouquet she would have been hard pushed to accurately describe yet, the moment she inhaled it, could recall with precision.

Tears trickled down the back of her throat; was this real? Afraid to open her eyes and prove she might be dreaming, she sat tight. Aware now of her back, her spine which felt soft and flexible, like she could run up and down the stairs for days! Gone was the creaking fragility to her bones, the lumbering encumbrance of immobile limbs, the tightness to her knuckles and joints that meant she feared falling. So brittle, she was certain she'd shatter like china on impact.

A wide smile formed on her mouth, where whole teeth, solid and sturdy in her plump gums now sat. Hesitantly opening her eyes, she placed her shaking hand over her mouth, before jumping up and walking to the mirror that hung over the fireplace in the front parlour of her childhood home. Her fingers touched her cheekbones, her lips. My goodness, she had been so young! Her skin like peaches and cream without a line, a wrinkle, a dent, a scar and no dark patches of sun damage through which poked obstinate bristles.

'How on earth?' It was at once wonderful, overwhelming and glorious!

She was here, at home on October 14th, 1940.

Dizzy with joy and disbelief, she noted the smoke from her breath as she exhaled in this chilly room where the meagre fire did little to warm the air and the coal barely glowed in the grate. It was sparsely furnished, a little more drab than she'd remembered, yet familiar. The two brown chairs with cream lace antimacassars draped on the back, and wide rounded arms, perfect for resting a book or cup of tea. A framed black and white picture of her unsmiling grandmother in her high-necked blouse sat on the mantlepiece. The rag rug in front of the fireplace, where a companion set of tongs, prong, brush and dustpan dangled from a polished brass stand.

The large radio sat on the end table and the embroidered footstool her mother had received when her great aunt Lily had died rested on the floor. Violet had quite forgotten that too. It was a room that lived in her memory as a place of colour, of joy! Yet the reality was a certain bleakness, a dour room really that could only benefit from central heating, bright paint, soft blankets, colourful cushions, and a couple of fancy lamps, which, of course, would all be available to whoever lived here, in time.

Part of the gloom, of course, came from the lack of streetlamps, the blacked-out windows and the shiver of fear that ran through every house in this country at war. Looking towards the door, she wondered if her mother were in the kitchen, and her heart stuttered with the desire to run to her mum! Chen's words came to her now, *'you can't leave the room, or you will find yourself at home.'*

Violet didn't want that, didn't want to waste a second, and so sat down again, sat very still, and waited. She ran her hand over her frock, one of two she owned, and the green, knitted cardigan she wore over the top, made by her mother's own hand. Lifting the hem, she raised it to her mouth and kissed the wool, inhaling it, recognising her own youthful scent in a time before deodorants and perfumes were readily available. Her tights were thick wool, and it was jarring to realise that the faint odour of a body in need of a good wash came from herself. These the days when bathing happened weekly, and hair was washed about the same. Her scalp itched with the need to feel the soft suds of a decent shampoo.

Then it came, the knock at the front door and her mother's voice! Her sweet, sweet mother, calling from the hallway,

'I'll get it!'

Balling her dainty fingers into a fist, she placed her knuckles into her mouth. Her mother was on the other side of that door, *her mummy*, long, long gone. It took all of her strength not to run to her, knowing to glimpse her, touch her, receive a smile, might well be worth losing her fifteen minutes.

'She's in the parlour, love. Hurry now, don't let the heat out.'

Violet smiled and wiped her eyes. God only knew how chilly it must be outside if this was considered heat. *Her mother* here, present, alive! Violet pictured her wrap around pinny and sturdy lace up shoes.

'Thanks, Mrs Bertram.'

Elsie's voice! Oh my goodness! *Elsie's voice!* It was all she could do to control the powerful surge of emotion in her chest.

Then almost immediately the twist of the door handle…

Just like that, it all came back to her. The last time Violet had seen her. Elsie had called around. It was a Saturday night, dark outside, and the two had a brief catch up, made a plan for the next day, to meet up after church and walk home the long way, nattering as they did so. Violet had gone to bed happy, excited, looking forward to seeing her best friend. She had slept deeply, woken when the siren assaulted her ears. Grabbing her gas mask and coat from the bed post, she'd met her mum on the landing and, in a well-practised manner, each trying to keep the other calm, they'd made their way out towards the Anderson shelter and felt their way down into the dark, sitting huddled together on the little bench, waiting for it all to be over. Their limbs quaking with fear at every rumble, every bang. Praying they were going to be lucky.

One such rumble and bang had occurred on Juniper Street where a sleeping Elsie Porter was not so lucky. Elsie, who had, not a couple of hours before, stood in Violet's parlour and made a plan. The Porter's suffered a direct hit. The house and everyone in it, Elsie, her mother, her younger brother, and older sister, all perished, laying like a bloody human jigsaw among the flaming remains and charred bricks that had been their haven. Just like that, destroyed. Gone was the house Elsie's father and brother dreamed of coming home to, while they battled in the very worst of conditions, fighting hard to protect the way of life of those at home.

'All right, Vi?' Elsie stomped her feet on the rug. 'God, it's taters out there!'

And there she was! Alive! Restored and beautiful!

Violet had forgotten just how beautiful. Her perfectly shaped lips, eyes twinkling with the mischief that was never far away from her thoughts. Her beloved friend, her very best friend, who was engaged to Harry Drummond.

Violet stood slowly and wrapped her in a warm, close hold. Their spare bodies colliding, without the pouch of stomach that had born three children or flesh worn loose on thin muscles, skin that drooped.

'Blimey, girl, what's got into you? Get off you daft apeth!' Elsie shoved her.

'Nothing, I just.'

'You been on the cooking sherry?'

They both laughed; it had been many a month since they'd seen or sniffed cooking sherry. Even the most basic staples were in short supply.

'Just pleased to see you!' she beamed. It was the truth. *A miracle! Magic!*

'Oh, my days! Well there's a welcome if ever I've 'ad one.' Elsie sat on one of the chairs and crossed her legs, removing her woollen beret and matching mittens, which she placed neatly on the arm of the chair. 'Still no letter.' She pulled a face.

Violet, with the wonderful benefit of hindsight, knew that Harry was in fact stationed in North Africa and that he wrote to Elsie regularly. She recalled the string-wrapped bundle that had been returned to him, unopened after the war. One of the only times she'd seen him cry.

'He will have written to you, I'm sure of it. He loves you, Els.' Her voice was soft, lilting, higher than she was used to without the aged growl that came from vocal cords that had lost their lubrication. It felt odd, reassuring another woman that she held a place in the heart of the man who was to become Violet's husband, but it was no less honest for that. It was the truth, Harry had loved Elsie, very, very much.

'Just want to know he's doing all right.'

'You know what they say, mate, bad news travels fastest.' This the phrase she used to placate herself in the wee small hours when her fear for her big brother and her daddy sometimes felt overwhelming. Her words tripping over the boulder of grief that sat at the base of her throat, knowing that her best friend, this darling girl, would never get to read Harry's words of love and longing written in a letter. But Violet had seen them, and they were beautiful.

The walnut clock on the mantelpiece ticked loudly, a reminder of the little time she had.

'I wanted to say to you, Els, if anything happened to me and if, if Harry didn't come home. I wouldn't mind if you went out with Cyril.'

Her friend let out a loud laugh and leaned forward, as if the very suggestion was absurd.

'First, ain't nothing going to happen to you or Harry,' her friend spoke prophetically, 'but, if it did, I don't want your Cyril!'

'He's not my Cyril, not really, we're pen pals more than anything.' She felt nothing romantically for the boy but knew her letters to him might lift his mood when he needed it most.

'Why? Are you saying you'd go after my Harry?' Elsie narrowed her eyes.

For Violet it was as if the air had been sucked from the room. She felt her face fall into a serious expression and turned to face her friend.

'I think he's,' she swallowed. What did she want to say, what *could* she say without belying their sixty years married, three children, five grandchildren, a solid little life lived in harmony, a life that would be denied Elsie who currently wore his grandmother's ring? A ring that would be lost in the rubble forever. 'I do think he's lovely, a lovely man, a good sort.'

Elsie reached out and took Violet's hand into her own.

'I think, Vi, me old mucker, that if anything happened to me then I would like nothing more than the two people I love most in the whole wide world to make each other happy.'

Violet felt the rush of tears and did her best to keep them at bay, as decades of remorse and shame lifted from her shoulders.

'Really?' her voice no more than a whisper, as she clutched Elsie's hand tightly.

'Really. But if *nothing* happens to me and you so much as go after a hair on his head, I'll knock your bloody block off!'

They laughed then, the two girls. One with so much life left to live and the other about to go to her final rest.

'I'd better go. Me mother'll be getting her knickers in a twist, you know what she's like about me being out in the dark, said I'd go straight back.'

As Elsie stood and restored her hat and mittens, Violet felt something close to panic, wanting so badly to tell her friend to stay the night, to sleep in the shelter, to empty the house! But Chen was right, it had already happened, and this was no more than a window, a brief peep back in time.

'I know we don't say it, but I d'narf love you, Elsie Porter.'

'Oh, you great big softie!' – her friend pulled her close – 'and I bloody love you. See you tomorrow. God bless.'

Elsie spoke with certainty, casually, as she reached for the door, turning briefly to face her friend for the very last time. There was a moment, a mere second when the smile on her face suggested she might have some small knowledge, the merest hint that all was not as it seemed.

'Yep.' Violet smiled back, doing her best to keep her tears at bay. 'God bless. See you tomorrow, Els.'

The moment her friend had gone, Violet staggered to the chair and sat, doing her best to catch her breath, to calm her flustered pulse. Closing her eyes, she let her head drop to her chest, exhausted by the seemingly unremarkable exchange, yet knowing it was the greatest, most wonderful, life changing thing! She wanted to tell the world, but who would believe her? She scarcely believed it herself.

It was as she lifted her head that she felt the pain in her lower back, and a heaviness to her being. To have been briefly free of it only served to remind her of how much her age ailed her.

Her tears fell freely then. A potent mixture of sadness for Elsie's young life wiped out in the blink of an eye and also something very close to relief, as the guilt of decades leeched from her bones.

Her best friend – her very best friend – had given Violet permission, and this was the greatest gift.

Looking up now into the starry sky overhead, she whispered through her tears, picturing Chen, wondering who he was and how, *how* it was possible! Hoping her words might spiral up into the night sky, find their way through the stars and land in his ear,

'Thank you! Oh my goodness, how can I ever thank you...'

Chapter Three - Lewis Mark Noble

Aged 36

Henbury, Bristol

Lewis stood in front of the open fridge staring at the less than inspiring contents that lurked on the glass shelves where stubborn fragments of salad leaves, now transparent, clung to the surface. Out of date jars of pickle and jam with equally sticky misaligned lids huddled forlornly in the door. He sighed. He was still learning. Eighteen months in and he was still learning.

How to make a meal out of nothing, something that Jane had always made look so easy.

How to wash and dry the laundry without it either shrinking and over baking in the tumble dryer or the sheets going back onto the bed with a faint and unpleasant dampness to them.

How to keep track of everyone's birthdays, anniversaries, house moves, christenings, engagements, exams, driving tests and weddings that all, it seemed, required the sending of a bloody card.

How to make the house feel cosy, the lighting not too harsh or too dim.

How to take care of the plants so he neither drowned and killed them or underwatered and killed them.

How to plump a cushion!

How to walk past the photograph of him and Jane on the wall by the front door without closing his eyes, unable to stand it, the image of them, smiling, happy, hopeful on the day of their wedding.

How to remember the names of all the neighbours and their kids. No longer was he able to click his fingers and say to his wife, 'you know, three doors down, Overly Keen Bin Bloke' – only for her to reply, 'Oh, that's Shaun, married to Marta.'

How to get the stains of slopped tea, engine oil and duck shit out of the pale rug. The tea and oil down to a potent combination of thoughtlessness and fatigue. The duck shit a gift from his brother who had trailed it from the park and right through their front door on the sole of his boot.

How to put up and decorate the Christmas tree without it inviting comedic insults from all who saw it, causing him to weep when alone at the ridiculousness of his efforts, and the powerful reminder of how beautiful his wife had made their home at that time of year. How beautiful she had made their home every day.

How to get through each day, go to work, function with a lance of grief skewering his heart and chest that made even taking a breath difficult.

Yes, he was still learning.

His wife had died eighteen months ago. It had changed him in the most profound ways. The sadness and loneliness he had expected, but he hadn't understood how every aspect of his life, belief system and routine would be ripped to shreds. It seemed as if he spent the majority of his time trying to figure out how to put it all back together.

Always of a practical mind and without any strong religious conviction, Lewis found himself pondering the Universe, looking for any kind of association to the 'other-worldly' and making links where there were none. This he did quietly, privately, without regret or apology, taking immense comfort from any perceivable sign. These included staring at a prominent cloud that looked vaguely tree shaped. Jane had loved trees, was this a sign? Smelling her favoured perfume in a crowded department store. Actually, *in* the perfumery, but lingering a while with his eyes closed, was this her too? And his particular favourite: spotting a large adult eagle hovering over the field near their house, and wondering if his wife might have returned as an eagle. It was comical, he knew. The fact that the bird was probably a few years old at least was neither here nor there.

That was the thing about grief. It wasn't rational, wasn't linear, and wasn't fair. It was instead a terrible journey that he, like most people, had been unprepared to travel, even though he had tried to ready himself for it as Jane's health faded and her death went from a terrible, unthinkable thing to a certainty. Ironically, the only person who would have made this journey more bearable if he'd travelled it with them, was Jane. His grief held him fast, usurped him at will. It was exhausting and changed the shape of him. It still struck him as odd that something so widespread and general could feel so unique.

'Eggs.' he spied the carboard box and pictured his options: on toast, scrambled, fried or poached. Or maybe an omelette? 'Bloody eggs.' He reached for the box and placed it next to the cooker. 'I've eaten so many bloody eggs, I wouldn't be surprised if I started sprouting feathers!' he gave a short laugh. He did this, chattered as if she was standing at the sink or sitting at the table and smiling along as he regaled the room with his interior monologue. The quiet that followed was always deafening, debilitating and made him sadder than he would ever care to admit.

His phone rang.

There it was, like clockwork. It was like the woman had a camera trained on him.

'Hello, Margaret.'

'Hi, love, it's me, Margaret.'

'Yep.' He closed his eyes and pinched the bridge of his nose between his thumb and forefinger, remembering to be patient. It wasn't that he didn't want to chat with his mother-in-law, he did, but it was more the irritating timing of her phone calls. Always, always when he was cooking, preparing or planning his supper. It just irked him!

'Work all right?'

'Yeah, you know, same old, same old.' He had long ago run out of ways to reveal non-existent highlights in his role as a forklift operator in a vast warehouse in Avonmouth. A monotonous job really but, with good pay and regular hours, he didn't like to moan about it. Well that wasn't strictly true. He used to like to moan about it quite a lot, actually, to Jane. She'd nod, smile or tut, smooth his brow, make him a cuppa and remind him that real life was what happened on this side of their front door and that everything outside was no more than a means to an end.

God, how he missed her!

There it was again, that tight feeling across his chest as if the air was too thin, as if he might actually drown on the tears that slipped wordlessly down the back of his throat, as his whole body shivered with cold that was nothing to do with the temperature. Margaret was still speaking; he felt guilty for having tuned her out,

'So that was good. Oh, and I saw Melissa today, she came over with the kids and they stayed for a bit. Millie has been to nursery, she's done you a picture – you could put it up in the kitchen. Little Noah's getting big, he tipped out my button box. Took me ages to gather them up and put them all away, some had rolled right under the sofa. There I was on my hands and knees gathering the little things up.'

'Huh!' all he could offer. He didn't care about Millie or little Noah or Melissa, his sister-in-law, didn't care about nursery, pictures for his kitchen or the button box – none of it. He just wanted to be left alone to miss his wife and cry quietly behind the closed curtains.

'I'm going up Cribbs at the weekend if you need anything, love.'

'Don't think so.'

Then came the awkward pause while she waited and he listened, both it seemed unsure how to fill the silence. It made him cringe. Every time.

'Right. Well. I'll let you go then, Lew.'

'Yep, see you later.'

'Yep. See you later.' She ended the call.

He exhaled with relief, thankful the irritating, pointless daily ritual was over. Opening the egg box he suddenly lost his appetite along with the desire to cook at all. Toast would do. Egg on toast without the egg.

Even he could manage that.

***

With his car parked, Lewis made his way to the security point, pass in one hand, rucksack in the other ready for searching. All standard procedure at the huge warehouse that was like a small city. Its vast proportions dominated the landscape in this corner of Avonmouth.

'Morning.'

'Morning.' He smiled at the smooth-skinned, smiley-faced man in front of him who had spoken over his shoulder. A newbie, he suspected, as no one who had been here a while and knew the ropes had such a joyful demeanour. That, and he hadn't seen him before.

'I was hoping to bump into you, actually,' the man now turned to face him, speaking with a familiarity that was a little unnerving.

'Oh yeah?' He wondered if the bloke were new to his section or had been drafted in by management. Either way, Lewis was riled, it was the last thing he needed, a change to his routine, a new initiative, more forms to fill in, or – the worst thought of all – having to train someone, engage with them. He wasn't keen on interacting with strangers. Jeez, he wasn't that keen on interacting with people who weren't strangers, not when his head was still so scrambled with grief and what he longed for most was solitude.

'It's Lewis, right?'

'Yep.'

'I'm Chen.'

'Alright,' he offered by way of greeting, racking his brain, trying to recall if and where they had met before.

'What I'm about to tell you, Lewis, will be surprising, unsettling even.'

'What you talking about?' He took a step backwards. The guy was right about one thing; he was already unsettled.

Chen began to speak, quickly, fluidly, sincerely, never breaking eye contact, his body relaxed, his manner assured with an undertone of urgency.

'I'll get to the point,' Chen smiled at him. 'The one thing I need to tell you, Lewis, is that I have never and will never tell you a lie…'

Never a violent man, Lewis listened to Chen spout his bullshit about time and felt his fingers flex into fists, quietly confident that, if they hadn't been on his work premises and he didn't need this job, the one bit of stability in his topsy-turvy life, he'd have shoved him hard and watched him fall on his arse. The prick! Did he look like the kind of person who would fall for such a scam? Not that he could figure out the bloke's angle – what was he after, money? Or maybe it was a hoax, considered funny when it was anything but. Who would put him up to such a thing? Gus in packing, possibly, or Mario in logistics, they both liked a laugh. Not that this was amusing, not even remotely. It bothered him, bothered him all day.

Driving home now after his shift, how he hated the lift in his sprits and the bunch in his gut at no more than the imaginary possibility of seeing Jane, touching Jane, feeling the presence of Jane.

What had the bloke said, *fifteen minutes,* my God! Fifteen minutes with her! What would he do, when would he pick?

It would be an easy decision. He'd choose the time before she got sick. Before pills, lotions, potions, pillows, medicine, rubber gloves, disposable aprons, tubes and the sincere words offered by medics invaded their bedroom and wrapped them in gloom. Before their room took on the slightly chemical smell of chemotherapy and he had no choice other than to tend to her like a nurse and not a lover. Before she lost the roundness to her cheek and the twinkle in her eye. Before he had to lift her diminished frame from the bed to the bathroom and back again. A journey of a few steps that left them both exhausted, beaten and so very sad. A marathon no less.

The traffic light turned red, and he stopped the car, hating the bloom of tears that threatened. No, there was nothing funny about anything Chen had said. It was like handing a starving man a lunch box with nothing in it or giving a poor man an empty wallet. It was cruel and made him want to punch the steering wheel. He might have done so too, if he wasn't in busy traffic and could have been confident that it wouldn't damage his motor.

The lights changed and he trundled home, wanting to arrive, but dreading, as he always did, the opening of the door into the darkened, quiet hallway.

Standing in the kitchen, Lewis tipped the tin of spaghetti hoops into the saucepan and watched the thick orange/red sauce start to bubble, just as the toast popped up.

And bingo!

His bloody phone rang. He turned the gas ring off and answered the call.

'Hello, Margaret.'

'Hi, love, it's me, Margaret.'

'Yep.' He took a deep breath, deciding in that second to forgo his planned supper and go straight to bed. He was tired. Too tired for spaghetti hoops.

'Work all right?'

'Yeah, you know, nothing to report.'

'I got a postcard today, from my cousin, do you remember me talking about Linda and Jeff?'

'No, I, not really.'

'They were at school together in Hartcliffe. Anyway, she got in the family way, and they married when they were ever so young. Her dad, my dad's brother, my Uncle Gavin, do you remember Gavin at your wedding? He was the one with the toy cat on the parcel shelf in the back of his car.'

'I, no, no, I don't.' He had no idea what she was wittering on about.

'Well, he was furious, as you can imagine, more or less marched poor old Jeff up the aisle in a borrowed suit. They was only babies themselves really, no more.' Margaret let out a small laugh, as if at the memory. 'Anyway, they're still together, nigh on forty-five years! Happy as larks they are. In't that lovely?'

'It is,' he managed, and there it was again, that flare of anger, underpinned with misplaced jealousy. How come Jeff and Linda got all that time when he and Jane had only been given six years. *Six measly years!* It wasn't enough, could never have been enough, even if they'd got a lifetime.

'Anyway, they've got a caravan in Mevagissey, and they sent me a postcard, in't that nice?'

'It is.'

And then it came. The awkward silence that made his teeth grind.

'Right. Well. I'll let you go then, Lew.'

'Yep, see you later.'

'Yep. See you later.' She ended the call.

Lewis leant on the countertop, arms outstretched, breath coming in gasps. He exhaled slowly. When would this get easier, when would he hurt less? He thought of Chen, the weird guy who had approached him in the queue and waffled on about time and his bizarre suggestion. He smiled, warmed at no more than the idea, what wouldn't he give for fifteen minutes with his girl.

***

It was Saturday.

Despite having slept for most of the day, Lewis toyed with the idea of going straight to bed and ignoring what the bloke had said. It was mad, he knew it. A ruse, impossible, a joke, and yet just the thought that it *might* be possible…

'You absolute plonker!' He took a sip from his can of Thatchers and settled onto the sofa, closing his eyes as the clock raced towards eleven. He knew he'd feel like an idiot when nothing happened, yet still felt the pull of attraction at no more than the imagining of it. Besides, what was the harm, no one would ever know.

With his eyes closed, he lay his head back on the cushion and waited, breathing slowly. Then came the oddest of sensations. The first thing he heard was a sound so glorious, so beautiful it took his breath away: his wife laughing. He'd almost forgotten it, the sweetness of it, as her laughter in the latter stages became wheeze riddled and forced, a throaty rasp that disguised only briefly what she was going through.

He opened his eyes immediately!

And there she was.

Oh!

His Jane!

His… his love!

Sitting on the end of the sofa, her legs curled beneath her, a cup of tea resting in her palms. She had her glasses on, her hair, still thick was piled messily on top of her head. She was wearing her pyjamas and the fluffy, pink socks her sister had bought for her birthday.

He daren't move, didn't want to break the spell.

My God, she was beautiful, *so beautiful!* To his horror he realised that he had forgotten some of the detail of her face. A realisation that hit him like a stone in the throat. The pain was sharp, and he swallowed. The small mole on the side of her chin had slipped entirely from his memory. The way her two front teeth were fractionally misaligned, meaning they rested by a millimetre on her bottom lip.

'What you staring at?' She pulled a face at him, a mock frown, as she kicked out with her socked foot to jab him in the thigh. Her blue eyes belied her delight, her joy!

'You,' he managed, heart racing, remembering what Chen had said, that he mustn't let on the reality of their interaction, and only had fifteen minutes.

He'd chosen this Saturday night, a few months before she got sick. They were watching TV, had ordered Chinese food that would be delivered in a little while. The last, ordinary, perfect evening in his memory, before a sudden pain and then the lengthy investigation and diagnosis that would send them into a tailspin. The last night they would make love without him being fearful of hurting her, causing her discomfort or inconvenience, before cancer eventually robbed them of that too. It was a hateful illness that took her piece by piece, dismantling their routine, their life and their future until he was all alone with an empty fridge and a desire to hide away with his sorrow.

Tentatively he sidled close to her, removed the mug of tea from her grip, placed it on the table and took her hand into his own.

'Oi! I was enjoying that!' she tutted before lifting their conjoined hands to her lips and kissing them.

Next, he muted the TV and sat as close to her as he could, shoulder to shoulder, thigh to thigh. Her head resting on the top of his arm. He inhaled the scent of her. She'd had a bath with those lemony scented bubbles that she loved. He breathed it in deeply.

'I love you, Jane,' he whispered, doing his best to keep the tremor of emotion from his voice.

'I know.' He could tell she was smiling, a fact that filled him with joy! The certainty in her response, the comfortable nature of their positioning. It was just as magical, as perfect as he'd imagined. 'My gentle giant!' Tilting her face, she kissed his neck. A kiss from those lips that had formed vows, spoken of love and made promises that he alone knew she would not – could not – keep. 'Do you want to watch a film?' she asked.

'No. I just want to sit here with you.'

It was the truth. This his greatest desire, a quiet moment of normality, side by side, as if they had all the time in the world. His understanding in that moment that this was what he had craved, and what he now mourned, the contentment of living a small, simple life with someone to love, who loved him in return.

'Spoke to my mum earlier.' His wife yawned and his heart flexed, that tiredness that dogged her, was this the start? Why had he not noticed, acted, done something! 'She breaks my heart. I know she misses my dad and tries her best to hide it. That's why she calls at tea-time, told me she can't bear to see the clock reaching six and not have him at the table with his tea in front of him. She misses having him to chit chat to about her day, the ordinary stuff. I know that's when she misses him the most. How sweet is that, but sad, right? I get it, though, when the rest of the street are feeding their loved ones and she's stood by herself in the kitchen, it's hard for her, d'you know what I mean?'

Lewis hadn't considered this. He felt a rise of something in his chest that felt a lot like guilt. The fact that his mother-in-law was still grieving her husband when her daughter had died, and that tea-time without her beloved was as hard for her as it was for him.

'Yes, I do know what you mean.' He made a silent promise to do better, be better for his mother-in-law who too lived in the shadow of loss.

Jane nestled closer into his form.

'You are lovely, Lew, the loveliest.' She kissed him again. This time he faced her, and her kiss landed on his mouth. His eyes, although closed, couldn't prevent the tears that graced his cheeks. To be kissed by her, touched by her, to feel her breath, warm against his skin.

'What you crying for, Bibber?'

He'd forgotten this too, she called him Bibber, he called her Babber.

'Just…' It was tempting, so tempting to tell her to go to the doctor tomorrow, or now, right now! To try and get the words out that she should rush to the hospital and tell them, tell them what? She didn't know yet. They didn't know yet. Besides, Chen had explained that one hint of forewarning and he'd lose this precious time, and he couldn't risk that, wanting to savour every single second!

He squeezed her hand, feeling the wedding and engagement rings roll against his palms, the same rings that now sat in a little glass pot on his bedside table.

'Just love you so much.'

'We're lucky, aren't we?' she whispered. 'Don't know anyone whose got what we've got or feel how we feel. I will spend the rest of my life loving you, Lewis Noble, loving you with my whole heart. What a lovely thing!'

He closed his eyes and wrapped her in his arms, knowing she spoke the truth. They were so very lucky, and it was indeed a fact she would spend the rest of her life loving him with her whole heart.

'It is, Janey, it's a lovely, lovely thing.'

The seconds ticked by, and he took the time to recall every facet of the way she felt in his embrace. Their hearts beating in rhythm, their breathing in sync. Content to sit here for eternity. He fought the desire to panic, to fret at no more than the thought that it was coming to an end.

'What was your favourite day ever?' he asked, holding her tightly, his voice hoarse with all it wanted to say and all he did his best to contain.

'Our wedding day,' she answered without hesitation. 'It was like time sped up and slowed down all at the same time. Even now, I often think about it. The way you looked, standing there waiting for me at the end of the aisle. The first time you saw my dress.'

'You looked like a movie star!'

'I felt like a movie star!' she chuckled that soft laugh that was like sunshine. 'Then kicking off my heels and dancing with the girls, sipping champagne. Uncle Tony falling down the steps of the hotel!'

'I'd forgotten that!' He had.

'Luckily his joints were lubricated with Guinness, and he didn't do any damage.'

'Only to the steps.' He laughed.

'Yep, probably. Mum crying all day, just sobbing with joy! Your dad hugging you and warning you to treat me right.'

'I hope I did, do... *do* treat you right, love.' He held his breath, waiting to see if he'd blown it, fearing she might disappear, and he'd be robbed of his remaining minutes. But no, it seemed he was permitted one small slip of the tongue.

'You know you do.' She squeezed his hand. 'And what about you, Lew, what was your favourite day ever?'

'This one,' he managed. 'This right now. Sitting here with you on the sofa. They don't tell you, do they, how it's the small things that are actually the big things. These quiet moments. They're what shape us, what bind us, aren't they?'

'They are, my love. They are.'

'I'm,' he took his time, forming his words, 'I'm so thankful for you, Jane. Can't imagine what I'd do without you.'

'Well, you'd miss me, of course, but you'd be fine.'

'Would I? You sound very certain.'

'Yes! Because you'd realise how lucky we were to have had each other and I'm sure – like me – you wouldn't trade the time we get for anything else in the whole wide world. Besides, it would do us a great disservice, wouldn't it, if the one left behind spent the rest of their time in misery and regret – that would be like taking a big chunk of our happiness and turning it into something else. Instead of celebrating the fact that we love each other no matter what. That would be a rotten thing to do. So yes, you'd be fine. And I'd be fine, if the boot was on the other foot. Eventually'.

'Eventually', he echoed.

It was when Jane trembled in his grip and his own body shook that he knew it was coming to an end.

And just like that, his arms were empty.

Still he sat, as though she were present, trying to conjure the warmth of her being against him. It had been the most beautiful, beautiful gift – and something he knew he'd never forget.

His tears – when they came – were not of the angry kind which he had grown used to but were instead tinged with something that felt a lot like joy. Happy tears! Because Jane, his beautiful wife, was right. Living a life cloaked in grief would be like taking a big chunk of their happiness and turning it into something else, what a rotten thing to do.

'Wow!' he wiped his face and spoke aloud into the ether, 'I don't know what to say, apart from thank you, Chen. Thank you!'

Lewis had slept soundly, this itself a rarity. Throwing open the windows of his bedroom, he stripped the bed linen to wash. Gathering his phone before heading out for a long overdue run, he put a call into his mother-in-law.

'Everything all right, Lew?' The note of concern in her tone was evident, and he understood. It was rare for him to get in touch.

'Yep, everything's fine, Margaret,' he smiled. 'I was just wondering if I could come and have me dinner with you tonight. I really fancy a home-cooked meal, or, more specifically, a home-cooked meal that is cooked by anyone other than me! Still not got the hang of it really.'

'Oh! Oh, Lew!' There was no disguising the emotion in her voice. 'That would be… that would be just marvellous! I'd love it! I'll get your favourite, a roast with all the trimmings!

I'll see if Melissa and the kids are free, they'd love to see you, I know.'

'Great. I'll see you later then.'

'Yes! Yes, love! I'll see you later.'

Standing now in front of the photograph of he and Jane on their wedding day, Lewis didn't close his eyes, but instead stared at her, giving silent thanks for the love they shared and would continue to share, no matter what.

Chapter Four - Ruby Jade Brown

Aged 23

Harborne, Birmingham

'See you Monday!' Ruby waved to the group of girls who stood arm in arm, high heels planted in puddles, hair worked loose from ties and blouse buttons undone, trying to counter the heat of the club.

'We love you, Rubes!' Daisy called.

Nadia chimed in with the same, 'Yeah, we love you!'

'Love you guys too!' she laughed as she climbed into the back of the taxi and buckled up.

These were the best nights. The ones that happened without too much planning or forethought. Nights when laughter was high on the agenda and nearly everything was funny! When she thought no further ahead than the contents of her cocktail glass, the music was loud and she could dance, arms aloft, eyes closed, her friends close by. Glorious moments of happy escape.

'Earls Court Road?'

'That's the one. Yes, thank you.' She always used the same minicab company, booking ahead, understanding there was safety in it. The familiarity. The routine. Plus, it made her mum happy.

'You know how you're getting home?'

'I do, Mum. Please don't wait up, there's no need. I'll see you in the morning.'

This, however, was a new driver, one she hadn't seen before. He smiled at her in the 'rearview mirror. A nice face, smiley.

'Do you mind if I open the window a bit?'

'Not at all!' he seemed friendly, accommodating.

She wanted to feel the cool air on her faco; not only was she overly warm but sitting still helped her understand just how much she'd drank. Not that she was sloshed, but she certainly felt the edges of her world softened and smudged by a boozy haze. This not bad thing, a moment of relief, distraction. A large glass of water before bed would sort her out. She did, after all, have a busy Saturday planned. A day of chores and admin that her life and role – in the HR department at the university – meant were hard to complete from Monday to Friday.

'Have you had a good evening?' his manner enquiring, friendly, his voice pleasant.

'Yes! Out with work friends. And at least I don't have to set my alarm tomorrow. That's one good thing.' She relished her sleep.

'It's Ruby, isn't it?'

'Yes.' She became more attentive, wary, as the man used her first name, asked for information. Even Mohammed after years of picking her up and dropping her off still called her Miss Brown, respected her boundaries. With her guard up, she spoke confidently. 'Mohammed usually picks me up.' She wanted to let him know she was a regular.

'Yes, Frank said. Mohammed and his wife are visiting their son in Manchester, I believe. Sorry you've got me, a poor substitute, I'm sure, but I promise to deliver you safely home.'

So he knew Frank, the controller. Knew Mohammed who liked to talk about his boy, who was about her age, studying in Manchester. She relaxed a little.

'My name is Chen.'

'Hi, Chen.'

Some minutes passed before he spoke again.

'Can I ask you a question?' he asked as the cab halted in the traffic.

'Sure.' She shrugged. I mean, why not, it'd help the journey go quicker. Besides there weren't many questions she hadn't been asked on a night out.

'Can I buy you a drink?'

'Fancy a dance?'

'Why's a pretty girl like you not out with her bloke?'

'Can I get your Instagram?'

'Wanna come home with me?'

'Why so sad? Come on smile! It might never happen!'

Ruby would stare at them knowingly, tight lipped and resolute. Because the one thing she didn't share was that it had happened. And not only had it happened, but it had robbed her of her smile, for a while.

Chen cleared his throat. 'If you could spend time with anyone no longer alive, who would it be?'

'Oh, that's a great question!' Ruby sat forward, this a most unexpected topic and something she liked, games. 'I suppose,' she tapped her long nails on her mouth, 'I'd have to go for Dr Maya Angelou. I would sit at her feet and soak up the wisdom of everything she said! That'd be some night.'

'You've read her poetry?'

'I have, but it's one of her quotes that I think about most days, it motivates me, helps me.' Why she felt the need to expand further to the stranger driving the cab would have been hard to explain, yet she did.

'Which quote?'

'We may encounter many defeats, but we must not be defeated.'

'I like that.'

'I like it too.' She smiled out of the window of the cab, watching the neon signs of fast-food outlets, vape shops and brightly lit convenience stores slide by as they motored on.

'Dr Maya Angelou,' he repeated. 'You like the idea of it, Ruby? Having that chance to chat to someone no longer here?'

'I do.' She nodded, staring now into her lap. 'Who wouldn't?'

'True.' He laughed. 'I have something I need to say to you.' His tone now solemn and, for that reason alone, quite alarming.

'I'd rather just sit quietly if that's okay, it's been a bit of a night and—'

'Ruby. I need to speak quickly. Please believe me when I tell you that I have never and will never tell you a lie.'

'Okaaay,' she replied with nervous laughter. This guy, no matter how intriguing, was starting to sound a little weird.

He held her eyeline in the rearview mirror.

'I can give you that gift, Ruby. I can give you fifteen minutes, not with Dr Angelou, sadly, but with someone you've lost, someone known to you. Your case is a little different, Ruby; you will have to interact with others – if you choose who I think you will choose. Remember they have no idea that this is your fifteen minutes, you can't tell them, of course. Can't tell anyone.'

Chen carried on speaking, laying out the rules and regulations of the most far-fetched scenario she'd ever heard. He was taking the game to a whole other level! In truth she was torn between wanting to laugh out loud, wanting to tell him to shut up, and equally curious about his proposition. She chose to sit quietly, letting him talk while she tried and failed to tune him out.

It was an odd encounter to say the least.

When the car came to a stop outside of her childhood home in Earls Court Road, it was with a potent mix of mistrust and confusion that Ruby slammed the taxi door. She was unnerved and undecided in how to handle the situation. It was tempting to call Frank and make a complaint, but even the retelling would sound weird.

The driver you sent, Frank, the guy called Chen, he was odd, nice enough, but odd. Talking rubbish about giving me time. I don't want him picking me up again, I want Mohammed.

What would be the point? Chen might get fired and then how would she feel? He hadn't been mean, inappropriate or rude, and she'd felt safe as they trundled the familiar route towards home. He was just a little… she ran out of negative words because, actually, she had quite liked talking to him, liked even more the possibility of having those fifteen minutes. Now wouldn't that be a crazy, wonderful thing!

'Granny Elwood.' She beamed as she put the key in the door, 'or my wonderful primary school teacher, Mrs Nichols. Or you, Dad?' her tears bloomed, as she looked up into the night sky, as the last of her joyful booze glow fell from her shoulders with the raindrops that now landed with splats on the path around her. 'I miss you, Daddy…'

'That you, love?' her mum called from her bedroom on the landing.

'Yep! It's me!'

'Did you have a nice time?'

'I did.' She kicked off her shoes and relished the feel of the cold wooden floor on her throbbing feet.

'See you in the morning, darling, God bless.'

Ruby knew her mum, as usual, would have been loath to go to sleep until she knew her daughter was safely home.

'That's the thing with daughters,' her mother had once explained. *'They're a little piece of your heart and, if you're not near them or can't see them or touch them, then it's a most uncomfortable state of affairs, like a piece of you is missing.'*

'See you in the morning, Mumma, God bless.'

Ruby ran the cold tap and grabbed a pint glass from the shelf. This something she understood. She too felt like a little piece of her was missing.

***

It was the next night and after a busy day, and with her mum sleeping soundly, Ruby gripped the banister and prepared to climb the stairs for bed.

'What if,' she whispered. Rolling her eyes at her stupidity and gullibility. Returning to the kitchen, she took a seat at the table.

She thought about Marvin, wondering where he was, what he was doing and absurdly wished he were sitting here with her. He was lovely, Marvin, but it wasn't meant to be. They'd had a wonderful time, not quite love, but she had no doubt that, with enough time and the dismantling of their walls, it might have been possible. It certainly felt like that was where they were headed. What they went through, while so young, would have been hard enough for even the most established couples to weather. They hadn't really stood a chance, still in the infancy of their relationship, as they tried to navigate the hardest thing of all.

Ruby had given it a lot of thought over the last three years, understanding that, when a loss was solely yours to bear, it was easy to reach out to those unaffected and lean on them for support, but, when that loss affected you both, affected you all, it cast ripples that would continue outwards until the end of time. Distorting the picture, fracturing the calm surface and making it almost impossible to connect at the level necessary for them to grow as a couple. Broken before they even started.

And here she now sat in the half light, the room bathed in the glow of the moon that shone through the kitchen window, as truly, without expectation or belief, she placed her palms flat on the surface where she had eaten a thousand meals, played hundreds of card and board games with her ailing dad, laughed over Christmas lunch with her brother, and wept on the day they'd said goodbye to her dad. All of it right here at this four-foot square of yellow Formica that was the centre of their world.

It was a strange sensation, as the clock struck. A juddering almost, a bit like an earthquake, or so she imagined. The blood raced in her veins and a plug of fear in her throat made breathing tricky. And then, instantly, everything was calm, and Ruby knew where she was, transported to a place, recognisable by no more than the sounds that both filled her dreams and fuelled her nightmares.

If you've never heard it, then lucky old you.

It would be hard to properly and adequately explain not only the noises, but, more importantly, the way they made her feel. She'd buried a lot of it, did her best to dismiss it from her thoughts. Evidently so as this sudden immersion took her right back to that day, that terrible, terrible day.

The room was reverentially silent like a place of worship, a description that wasn't entirely inaccurate. The quiet punctuated only by the symphony of beeps, blips, buzzers and bells. Complicated machinery that kept tiny hearts beating and impossibly small lungs inflating. It was overwhelming, to be there among the sterile, shiny, invasive equipment, all designed to keep the blood of the most fragile, tiny people pumping around their bodies.

Her own heart thumped with the same level of anxiety she'd felt on that day.

The air of the NICU carried a particular weight, which was little to do with the overly warm, oppressive temperature, entirely necessary, of course. But more the expectation and prayers of everyone present exhaled into the small space. It was as if she could taste the sorrow, could breathe in the hope and longing. The mental negotiating of deals that would never be done, and yet, everyone tried hard.

'Take me instead, let it be me, give him a chance!'

'Let her live, I'm begging you! I just want her to have the opportunity to grow and live and breathe and succeed and be happy! Oh for her to be happy! Please, please!'

'I will never ask for anything again, not ever! I just want to see her first nativity, first day at school, her wedding day. I want to see it all, please, please, please, please...'

'Not him, not him, not him, not my most precious boy! Save him!'

Those who sat patiently by the side of the plastic incubators could barely meet each other's eye. Ruby understood. Remembering how she had stared at those tiny babies, praying with every fibre of her being, hoping it was not her baby who succumbed. Horrendously and unthinkably navigating the thought that, if one had to go, then please, please let it be another person who was handed that small, wrapped bundle. Watching helplessly, as machines were unplugged, voices lowered, and prayers whispered sensitively into the ether. Wanting the wail of distress to come from another mother, meaning it was not her turn, anything but that!

Oh what a truly sorrowful and most desperate state of affairs.

Ruby had prayed constantly, prayed day and night for a miracle. The doctor had been kind, yet blunt,

'I would say that her chances are slim. I'm so sorry, Ruby, but I think you need to accept that she is very, very poorly and only getting weaker. If it wasn't for the interventions that are helping to keep her here, then…'

'Is it better we let her go, is she in pain?' Marvin had asked, and she'd wanted to leap at him, claws out, chest heaving, a rage of anger and distress ready to spew from her.

'Don't you dare say that! Don't you dare, Marvin! We will fight for her; we will fight with her!' she'd screamed.

He'd stared at her, eyes wide, his face so desperately sad, 'But what if she doesn't have any fight left Ruby? What if she's tired and just wants to rest. What if she wants to go home?' he whispered.

'Get away from me!' she had responded, standing up straight, resisting the urge to fall to the floor and beat her fists as she wept. 'Get away from me!'

That exchange had proved the beginning of the end. The two youngsters worlds apart and without the history or depth of foundation to find a way forward. Strangers really who were forever bound by this life changing thing.

The last days had understandably been the worst. Indelibly etched in her thoughts and still with the power to shake her from sleep in the early hours.

There appeared to be little physical change in her daughter's condition, but there was a conversation when a nurse had come into Ruby's room, opened a window and the warm air had rushed out into the world along with the last remaining vestiges of hope.

The nurse's words had echoed, as if delivered under water. And Ruby, submerged in a sea of sadness and fatigue had done her best to decipher them.

Three years had passed, and she was still trying to make sense of it all. The nurse, whose face she could picture, but name she couldn't recall, stood by the side of her bed.

'The thing is, Ruby, this might be your last chance.'

'I don't, don't want to, don't want to hold her or say goodbye. I, I can't!' The thought of her baby slipping away in her arms, the idea of watching her take her last breath, how could any mother agree to that? It was a feeling deeper than fear.

'I know you say that now,' the nurse had carried on, speaking quietly, yet undeterred, 'and I'm not in any way trying to coerce or encourage you into a decision, but I can give you the benefit of my experience and tell you that, sadly, I've been here many, many times before. More times than I would care to count, and every single person who has taken the chance to hold their little one and say goodbye has found comfort in it.'

'I can't do it.' She'd shaken her head resolutely, wishing that Marvin were there, wishing she hadn't sent him away. Wishing so many things…

'I can't imagine what you are going through, dear. But I do think the comfort it brings, holding her, might not be immediate, but might help you find peace in the future. I know this because those people, the mums and dads, they write, and they tell me. They say they have no regrets, and that it helped.'

'I'm not those people.' Ruby might be young, but she knew her mind, knew what action she needed to take, to get through this, to survive.

'True, everyone's different.' The nurse's tone was kindly, 'It's your decision, Ruby.'

She nodded, unable to admit that it felt almost impossible to make the decision with every fibre of her being in pain. Her skin inflamed, her limbs cumbersome, her brain foggy, heart breaking and her thoughts wild.

'I think if I don't see her at the end, don't touch her, then I can picture her in that little plastic cot, but still here. It'll be easier to handle, easier to forget the end. Easier to forget it all.'

'But maybe holding her, saying goodbye might make it easier to remember her?' the woman gave a half smile.

'I don't want the image of her, the knowledge of her, the scent of her, the feel of her against my skin. I don't want it. I can't cope. I can't, I can't! I'm supposed to go home with my baby, not hold her and watch her take her last breath and, then what, hand her over to who? How would I do that? And where will they take her, what then?'

She had shaken her head at the horror that lurked in her thoughts.

'Okay, Ruby. Okay.' The nurse had then pulled the top sheet on her bed taut, patted her on the leg and left the room with a long, lingering look over her shoulder, which Ruby caught. A look that was silently pleading yet understanding too.

It was the most horrific of situations, something she could never have imagined. Her pregnancy had been a surprise. Actually, not a surprise, a shock. She and Marvin, acquaintances at best. She fancied him. Liked his company. He made her laugh. But did she love him? No, she barely knew him. Did she envisage a future with him? No, nothing like that. They'd simply made a mistake, a drunken mistake, which had been fun and frivolous, nothing more. Until it was something so much more, the truth staring at her as she held those two plastic oar shaped sticks in the bathroom, having unceremoniously peed on them. Knowing, before those little lines of confirmation popped up in the small result window, exactly what would be revealed.

She might only have been nineteen but understood her body well enough to know what missed periods, sore boobs and that awful metallic taste in her mouth, meant. Telling her mum had been the hardest of all, and, to her eternal shame, it was a relief that her dad wasn't around to be part of the fiasco, to see his face crumple in disappointment the way her mum's did.

'Not my Ruby, not my little girl, not clever, clever you! You're going to university, you're going to do great things, take over the world! That's what you've worked so hard for! This foolishness is what happens to other people, silly girls who are careless, who don't know how to take care of themselves! Not you, Ruby!'

Turns out that was Ruby. She was silly and careless and didn't know how to take care of herself. But she was determined to figure out how to take care of her baby. At least in that regard she could step up to the plate and do a great thing. University would wait, but she'd still make it, she was sure. Plenty of other women did it, it was all about timing and planning, she'd figure it out.

The pregnancy had passed in a bit of a blur. Marvin did his best, shifting from one foot to the other at awkward hospital appointments where medics discussed her body as though he were familiar with it, and not just a boy who happened to have got caught in this pantomime.

'It's okay, Marv, you don't have to come in with me.'

'I want to. I do!' he'd nodded sincerely. Sweet, well brought up, kind, well intentioned Marvin, a good man, a good man who had gone on to marry Genevieve, and they'd moved away.

It was actually a relief knowing she wasn't going to bump into him in the supermarket or see him in the street or have to sit next to him on a bus or in church. All of it a relief. He was gone, married to someone else. Genevieve's husband now, and Ruby didn't have to think about him or being pregnant or anything that had come after.

Instead of *going* to university, a little frail, a little changed, she had decided to stay at home and now *worked* at the university, a simpler life. An easier life.

That's what happened when you had a breakdown. For her, at least. It had felt almost impossible to get back on track, to concentrate in the way she needed. And so she imagined a different future, watching other students fulfil the dreams that had once been hers.

The changes had all started right here, in the NICU.

Turns out the nurse was right. She had regretted not holding her child, not saying goodbye to her daughter. It had actually made things much harder for her, not having the scent, the memory, the imprint of Sahara on her skin. Sahara, that was what she named her, her baby girl, *their* baby girl. Sahara Rose Brown.

'There you are, Ruby.'

The nurse spoke as if she had only seen her minutes ago and not as if years had passed.

'Here I am.'

She smiled at a nurse whose face she'd forgotten, but yes, familiar as someone who worked in the NICU and who she now recognised. Her manner, efficient, on high alert. Her tone, blunt. Fingers, nimble, as she watched and listened. Moving and shifting wires and tubes, settling tiny limbs, stroking skin, administering drugs, speaking phrases of reassurance, placing woolly hats, doing everything and anything on her watch to make sure those little hearts kept beating and those lungs kept inflating, and the blood in those veins so visible under thin – so very thin – skin, kept pumping around those tiny bodies.

'Would you like to visit Sahara?'

Ruby nodded.

'You know the drill, let's get you scrubbed up!'

The memory of this too had dimmed: heading into the ante room with the big sink and the antiseptic hand soap. The particular way she had been shown to wash and dry her hands, the pulling on of the rubber apron and gloves when needed. The reminder of the pneumonic emblazoned on a poster: THANKS – Think Hands And No Kisses! These babies had immature, compromised immune systems and were susceptible to infection. Hands had to be scrupulously clean, and kissing the little ones on the face was a no-no.

It was as surreal as it was emotional, to be guided towards the plastic incubator where her little girl slept.

'Oh! Look at her!'

Sahara looked so tiny, reminding her of a little bird with her big eyes and translucent skin, the small, striped hat that kept her warm.

Ruby's nipples tightened with the need to feed and the unmistakeable pull of her womb, the throbbing ache of loss in the nest that had nurtured this little girl, also sensations she had almost forgotten.

'She's so beautiful!' she managed through a mouth contorted with emotion.

'She is,' the nurse confirmed. 'Would you like to hold her?'

Ruby stared at her baby.

'Would you like to hold her?' the nurse asked again.

'I think I would.' Her voice no more than a whisper, as she sat in the chair placed by the side of Sahara's crib.

'That's it, love, get comfy.'

Ruby shifted on the plastic-coated chair and did as she was asked. Then, without too much planning and none of the gentle, hesitant care that she had assumed might be the nature of the task, the nurse lifted Sahara from her crib with confidence. Handling her as if she were robust. The woman, adept at the task, managed not to tangle the many wires and tubes as she did so.

The nurse checked the baby over before placing the tiny doll-like creature in Ruby's arms and tucking a soft, pale blue blanket around her, to keep her snug.

'Oh!' Ruby stared at her daughter, whose eyes were closed, sleeping. Her narrow chest, tiny, tiny fingers, all so impossibly small! The weight in her arms, negligible.

'Hello, you, hello, darling!' Lowering her face, she inhaled the scent of her daughter. She placed her cheek against the top of her bobble hat and felt the warmth.

'Hello, it's me, your Mama,' she whispered.

There might have been a tiny flicker on her baby's face, movement of some kind. It was hard to tell, but, either way, Ruby knew this was the most precious fifteen minutes of her entire life, and how very thankful she was for the chance!

'I love you, Sahara, and I'm so sorry it took me so long to be here. I want to tell you that we are going to do so many great things.' As her daughter lay in her arms, Ruby allowed herself to imagine a different ending to the story for them both. 'We are going to have the best time together. I'm always going to be so proud that you're mine. I'm going to take your hand and show you the park. We can feed the ducks and walk along the canal.' It was then that her voice broke, and her tears came. 'I'll help you through your days at school and those tricky teenage years, when girls can be cruel, and boys can be tough to figure out and life can feel a little overwhelming. I know it was for me. You never have to worry about a thing, because I'm your Mama and I'll be right here for you. You can tell me anything and I will always believe you. I'll make you feel better when that boy breaks your heart.'

Ruby, sobbing now, sniffed at her tears, not wanting her vision clouded, not wanting a single moment of this interaction spoiled. 'Your daddy, Marvin. He's a really, really good man, a great man with kindness running through his bones. One of those people who does the right thing, and, even though he and I might not work out, he will always do the right thing by you, by me too. I can see that now.' Ruby paused and lifted her baby girl higher until she was almost resting on her chest. It was easier to smell her, see her and feel her. 'I want you to know that your little life might not have been planned, but you are no less longed for. And no less loved.'

Sahara lay still, like a tiny dormouse, at peace, contented, safe in her arms. It was wondrous to see, to feel. 'When you were in my tummy, I used to lie in bed and run my hand over the bump you formed, telling myself that you were an absolute miracle. I was never going to give up the chance to be your mummy. And I am your mummy, Sahara, I'll always be your mummy! Whatever comes next, I will always be your mummy, and you will always be my baby girl.'

It was then that emotion threatened to overwhelm her, and Ruby felt a slight shake to her body, understanding that her time was coming to an end.

'I will see you again, my sweet child. My daughter. My first born. You are a little piece of my heart. And if ever you're not near me or can't see me or touch me, then know it will be like a bit of me is missing. Until I see you again, Sahara, until I see you again…'

With a jolt, Ruby found herself back at the table in the kitchen where there was a chill in the air. Placing her head on the cradle of her arms, she cried. These tears felt different, as they were flavoured with relief.

'Ruby?' – her mum stood in the doorway in her dressing gown – 'Whatever is the matter child?' Her mother walked over and palmed circles on her back, just the proximity making her feel better, in the way it did with mothers and daughters, a connection most precious, unbreakable.

Ruby buried her head in her mother's hold as her mum took her in her arms.

'There, there, baby girl, it's all right…'

'We may encounter many defeats, Mumma, but we must not be defeated.'

'Amen!' her mother smiled. 'Amen.'

'I need to live for both of us, Mum. I need to live for myself, and for Sahara too. She never got the chance, but I will live for us both. I'm going to follow my dreams and do it for us both!'

'What are you going to do, Ruby?' her mother took the seat opposite her at the small, square table.

'I'm going to apply for a place at university. I'm going to chase it all. I'm going to try.'

'Ruby!' Her mum reached out and took her hands into her own, 'I am so happy right now! It's like my old Ruby is back! You *can* do it all, darling! I believe in you. What a change! How have you made this decision, how did you get here?'

'Oh, Mum, it sounds crazy!' – Ruby wiped her tears on the back of her hand – 'But would you believe I got here in a taxi, driven by a man called Chen?'

Chapter Five - Verity Louise Clarke

Aged 36

Morningside, Edinburgh

Verity collapsed her umbrella, shook off the droplets and rested it in the corner of the waiting room, knowing she would undoubtedly need it at the end of the day. Having stomped her sturdy brogues on the welcome mat, she tousled her short, damp hair with her fingers.

'Quick, the boss is in, look busy!'

It made her smile in the way Janice's quips often did.

'Morning, Janice.'

Their brilliant receptionist was a walking catalogue of cliches and catchphrases – enabling Verity to almost predict what she might come out with in any given situation. She was also a fixture, having been here for more years than Verity.

'Morning, Tara.'

'Morning! Coffee?' Janice's sidekick beamed from behind the reception desk they shared.

'Please, Tara. That'd be great. James not in yet?' She wanted to talk to him about their rota, as her fiancé, Patrick, was now working nights at the hospital, and she wanted to switch some of her days. There'd been mention of a possible trip to the coast for a beach walk and a pub lunch the week after. Both sounded very tempting, a trip out of the city.

'Not yet, he's got a few childcare issues this week, Mrs Scott is in Dubai.'

'Oh, yes, I forgot.' It amazed her how he did it, handled two small kids, a busy career and a very distracted wife.

'This weather, eh?' Janice shook her head, as if it was a shock to find herself in rain, in Scotland, in October. 'I'm absolutely drookit!'

'You need a brolly, I've told you before.'

'Aye, but with my shopping bag in one hand and my ciggie in the other, how would I manage a brolly?'

'You could always give up smoking?' It wasn't the first time she'd made such a suggestion, which made the woman roar as if it were that funny.

'I'd rather get wet!' Janice chortled. 'Besides, you know what they say.' Verity braced herself for a classic Janice comment. She was not left disappointed. 'Today's rain is tomorrow's whisky!'

'They do indeed.'

'First patient is in at eight. Mr Lowther.'

‘Ah, Mr Lowther.’ She nodded her understanding and walked into her consulting room. After hanging up her mac, smoothing her tweed skirt and taking a seat at her desk, she fired up the computer. She loathed the infernal machine, which took up more of her time than actual patients.

Such was the life of a modern G.P.

It baffled her dad, Dr Rodney – only recently retired – who liked to remind her that, in his day, everything had been written by hand and stored in a paper filing system. This, he insisted, was not only efficient and cheap to upgrade but was also very green and immune from hacking and glitches! He made it sound idyllic, those early days at his surgery in the rural Highlands, where Verity had grown up.

As the local doctor, he had tended to generations, and he, his wife and their two daughters were known by all. Verity tried not to think about her time there, finding it too painful to revisit. Memories that had the power to take her right back to those dark, dark days of grief.

Her lovely dad, despite their life changing tragedy, spoke fondly of the community. The vast landscape, a place of harsh weather and immeasurable beauty, where everyone pulled together to face whatever came their way, looking after each other, like family, protecting their own. If one of Jon Morton’s cows needed help delivering her calf, or snow saw the school cut off from the road, power out, it was all hands on deck!

She'd told him that if he helped birth a cow now he'd probably get sued.

'World's gone mad!' his favourite refrain, uttered usually as he shook invisible creases from his broadsheet and sighed. Verity found it hard to disagree but would privately add the caveat that their world went mad a long time ago, on the day they lost her big sister, Gracie, who would forever be seventeen.

They'd moved away soon after, settling here in Edinburgh, starting over without the community that had felt like family. Here in the city where they were of no particular interest, just new faces in the crowd, but, in the village they'd left, they were and always would be, the Clarkes whose wee girl was murdered.

Verity whizzed through her email, deleting great swathes of junk without reading it, mainly adverts in the form of 'breaking news' from various drug companies. Conference organisers offering her early bird rates for events in far flung corners of the globe, and various procedural updates and admin demands from the NHS trust.

Her theory was that, if any of it was that important, they'd email again, or call her. She responded better to a phone call, as only a handful of people had her telephone number, and she only called those who mattered to her. It was a stark reminder of how few people did matter to her. Her dad, of course, her cousin Darius, his wife Gilly. Her best friend since high school Megan, her boyfriend Patrick, and Dottie.

Although the likelihood of Dottie calling her was very slim, being that she was a pampered whippet and all.

'Your coffee.' Tara breezed in and put the floral mug on her desk.

'Thanks, Tara, I'll return the favour in an hour or so.'

'No worries, and Mr Lowther is here,' she whispered, pulling a wide-mouthed face.

'Of course he is!' Grabbing the mug, Verity took a large gulp of coffee, not knowing when she might next get the chance. 'You know the drill. If it looks like I'm stuck, make the call. And if he's still here by tonight, send in gin.'

'Got it!' Tara laughed and closed the door behind her.

Verity didn't like having the contingency in place, wished she could give every patient who walked through her door all the time they needed, but, alas, she was on the clock and, even though they might not know it, so were her patients. Every day was a race, as she did her best to get through her list, make phone calls, follow up on appointments, relay results, deal with any emergencies, chase various departments at various hospitals for updates and, if she were very lucky, grab a bite of a sandwich for lunch.

There it was, the sound she heard in her sleep, the knock on her door.

'Come in!'

'Morning, Doc.'

'Mr Lowther, nice to see you. Please, take a seat!'

He did as instructed while she pulled up his notes. More of a novel than notes – she idly scrolled through the familiar pages and pages, listing his various ailments from A to Z.

'What can I do for you today?' placing the emphasis on the word 'today,' hinting subtly at the fact she had seen him only two weeks ago and that he would undoubtedly pop in again before the month was out. Folding her hands on the desk top, she braced herself.

'I'm no feeling great. The wife says I'm lookin' a bit peely wally, thought it best to come see you.'

'Mr Lowther, are you feeling sick or is it more like flu or do you have any particular pain? Is there an area you would like me to concentrate on? If I can get a rough idea of the issue before I examine you, that would really help. Could you be a bit more specific?'

'No really.' He sniffed, as if her line of questioning was inconvenient.

'Okay, so, if you had to describe the problem, or the problem that's causing you the *most* concern, what would you say?'

It was always preferable to see Mr Lowther early in the morning when her tolerance had not been eroded by the fatigue of a long day.

'I reckon it's all of it.'

'All of it?' She'd lost the thread.

'Aye, everything you just said, I feel sick, there's a bit of flu and generally I'm in pain. Kinda, all over.'

Verity opened her mouth to speak, but paused, quite unsure where to go next. Wondering if she dare suggest they get right to the point, and she sign him off from work. She was, quite rightly, unhappy to make the assumption or take the risk, just in case.

'Right, well first things first.' She reached for her stethoscope. 'Let's have a listen to your chest.'

After Mr Lowther's extended stay, the morning passed quickly.

Verity nipped to the loo and hurried back to her desk. No sooner had she restored her glasses than there was the knock on her door. A quick glance at her computer told her it was Mrs Brooks, who was twenty weeks pregnant with her third child.

'Come in!'

And so it continued…

It was at the end of the day, as she gripped the handle of her umbrella and smiled at the cleaner, that Verity noticed the man in a dark suit, holding a briefcase and standing at the bottom of the path. It was her route to the main road and the bus stop where she would hop on the bus that would deliver her home. She left the surgery, hoping he might move. He didn't.

'Dr Clarke, hello.' His smile was wide. He looked healthy, certainly not in urgent need of medical care that she could see. She didn't recognise him, but that wasn't unusual.

Having seen so many people over the years, many only briefly, it wasn't unheard of for patients to recognise Verity while they remained strangers to her.

'Hi,' she replied, wondering if she should loiter and wait for James. This too was part of her life as a G.P, having to be wary of anyone who might be a little unintentionally invasive. It wasn't uncommon for a toxic combination of frustration and poor mental health to erupt in anger misdirected at her. People wanted her to have the answers. And as someone who lived without answers, she understood their irritation, but was still wary of putting herself in the line of fire.

'I was wondering if I might have a word with you?'

'Oh,' instantly on guard, she looked back at the surgery door, as if she might be able to summon James with no more than a thought. 'I'm actually in a bit of a rush; what I'd suggest is that you call the surgery first thing in the morning and make an appointment, we can—'

'No, Verity, it's not a medical matter.'

'Do I know you?' It wasn't only the confidence with which he'd used her name, but also his manner, clear voice and earnest expression that pulled her in.

'My name is Chen.'

'Hello, Chen.' She swallowed, looking from the road to the surgery door, still undecided which way to walk should the need arise.

'Please don't be alarmed.' He spoke the words that were almost guaranteed to alarm her. 'I'm here to give you a message, if you will.'

'I see. Well, as I said—'

'Verity,' again he used her name, and leaned forward, as if trying physically to put himself in the driving seat of their conversation. It was as bizarre as it was infuriating, the fact he had a message at all, a weird statement in itself. His whole manner was a little off. 'I spoke to your mother once, a long time ago now, Rosemary.'

Verity took a beat and studied his face.

'You spoke to her how, when?' It was jarring, hearing the name of her beloved mum who had passed away a decade ago, but mentally had more or less checked out when Gracie died. Her dad had picked up the mantel, tried his best, and how Verity loved him for it.

'We'll muddle though, won't we, hen? And muddle through they had.

'I visited her,' Chen stated.

'When she was sick?' She was interested, certainly.

'Not exactly.' His lack of specifics was beyond irritating. 'She wanted to talk to me about Grace.'

Verity shook her head and her stomach bunched. It was nonsense, of course, yet no less upsetting. And almost convincing. There was, however, a fatal flaw in Chen's ruse, in that her mother never went by the name Rosemary, her given name, which the press had printed. She was always, and only, ever known to her family, as Kiki.

A childhood nickname that had stuck.

'Look, I have no interest in what you have to say. I've had a very long day, and I need to get home, please,' her patience now edged with suspicion and irritation.

It wasn't hard for anyone to look up the details of her life online, to learn that her mother had passed away, to read of her sister's murder. To study the horrific detail of their family tragedy laid bare for all to see. Terrible, intimate details that every mother, father and sister would prefer not to have digitally captured for eternity, not that there was a damn thing she could do about that.

It was still of interest to people, her sister's killer never caught.

There'd been a party in a field, drink was taken, a fire built, the music was loud, and the next morning Gracie's naked body was discovered, discarded by the side of the road. A local boy, a cocky, rabble rouser named Dale McCurdy, had been the prime suspect, but there'd been very little to link him to the crime, other than a tidal wave of gossip. Plus, he had a solid alibi that put him fifty miles away for the whole night, which meant no one had ever had to answer for the crime.

It was one of the main reasons her parents had moved away. Not only to give Verity a fresh start away from the whispers, but also, and something she now understood, the prospect of bumping into McCurdy in the store or in the village was more than either of them could cope with.

Every so often, usually on the anniversary of Gracie's death, *five years... ten years...* a keen reporter would stumble across the file and rehash the story. Writing fresh, salacious copy to sit alongside the ghastly photo they always used: a stern-faced Gracie in black and white, looking nothing like the girl Verity remembered. Nothing like her wonderful big sister.

She had, in recent years, toyed with the idea of giving better photos to the newspapers, but Patrick helped her understand there was value not only in the fact that the girl in the image looked nothing like her sister, making the picture easier to face, but also the precious and private photographs that the family held were just that, precious and private. He was right, of course.

The world might think they knew Gracie's story, her name synonymous with a grisly end, gossip and spicy supposition, but the girl who lived in Verity's mind, who played the cello, sang like an angel, laughed like a drain, and had the most beautiful, beautiful mane of long red hair, well, that girl was hers alone.

Gracie's broken head had broken her parents' hearts.

It was that simple.

'Please excuse me, I need to,' she made to walk past Chen, who took a step to the side, clearing the path.

'Your mother told me to call her Kiki. I didn't ask her why.'

Verity stopped walking. And with her back to the man, she now listened with a growing sense of ease and curiosity.

'She also said you put something very specific in your sister's coffin, something of yours that meant a great deal to you, something that brought you comfort when you were a child, and that you hoped might do the same for Gracie. I only mention it not to be insensitive or to break a confidence, but to give you proof that I am who I say I am, and that I will only ever tell you the truth.'

My, my penguin. My stuffy, a soft-bellied little fella with stitched eyes and flat orange feet. He'd lived on my bed for the longest time. I'd hold him when I fell asleep...

'It was a penguin,' Chen almost whispered.

What the actual...

There were to her knowledge only four people in the whole wide world who knew about that, and two of them were dead. She turned now to face the man who had her full attention.

'How, how did you...'

'It's okay to be a little bit scared, Verity. I see this a lot, a natural reaction. Especially in this mistrustful world of ours, I understand. But I promise you that I have never and will never tell you a lie.'

'What is it you want exactly?' she gripped the brolly, doing her best to steady the tremble to her hands.

'I want you to listen to what I have to say. Five minutes of your time – that's all – and then I will go, and you'll never see me again. Can you do that?'

'Right here.' She stood her ground, banging the tip of the brolly onto the path, happy that James was inside the building and would make an appearance soon enough. 'You can talk to me right here.'

'Thank you,' Chen smiled, 'thank you.'

The bus wended its usual route. Verity sat by the steamed-up window, a little lost to her thoughts. The man, Chen, was mad, no doubt, but even she, a woman of science, could see how easy it would be to fall for such a story. There was seduction in it, no denying. It was deeply attractive, the thought of having fifteen minutes with someone she'd lost. Of course she would choose Gracie, of *course* she would.

Her sister had been just three years older than her when she died, yet the difference in life experience between fourteen years of age and seventeen was a gulf. It would forever be hard to reconcile that Gracie was now nearly twenty years younger than Verity, her baby sister. An age gap that would only grow as one of them grew older and the other did not. Verity would love just a glimpse of the girl she was, carefree, funny and clever, before she was made famous by that ugly black and white picture.

'Shit!' The bus stopped, and it was only the sight of her local coffee shop through the open door that made her realise it was her stop. Standing on the pavement, she took a minute, breathing deeply, trying and failing to make sense of it all. How had he known about her penguin? How had he known about any of it? That was the question.

***

Saturday night, and Patrick pulled his waxed jacket over his scrubs, before bending down to kiss her, 'ships that pass in the night!'

'See you in the morning.' Reaching up, she ran her palm over the side of his handsome face, thankful for this man of hers.

'See you in the morning, my love.'

'Be safe, rest if you can.'

'Huh, fat chance of any rest, but I'll certainly keep safe.' He kissed her again and headed out.

Dottie whined her disapproval.

'I know, Dots, but your dad's got to go to work. He needs to make all those people better who turn up pished and injured in the A&E! But next week – I promise you – it will be fun. We're off to the beach, in the rain, we'll get chips.'

Megan had called earlier, suggesting they meet for a drink or slump on a sofa and eat greasy noodles. Verity had politely made her excuses.

'I'm just not feeling it, Megs. It's been quite the week. I need ma bed! Please don't hate me.'

'Too late for that, I've hated you for years!'

They'd both laughed, theirs the kind of friendship that went far beyond feeling aggrieved by a declined invitation.

With Dottie snoring loudly in her basket in the kitchen, Verity switched off the lamp in the sitting room and went to grab her Kindle. It was almost impossible for her to sleep without reading something.

The screen glowed. Her eyes were drawn to the clock in the corner. It was nearly eleven. Standing in front of the window with the pretty view of honey glow streetlamps and chimney pots, she threw her head back and closed her eyes.

'What *are* you doing, Verity?' She shook her head, allowing a small burst of laughter to escape her lips at the utter absurdity of the situation. 'I will never tell a living soul about this!' she chuckled, as she slumped down on the rug by the window and, with her legs folded beneath her, closed her eyes. Doing her best to relax, it was hard not to blush with sheer embarrassment that she was giving this any credence at all!

Her memories of the weekend Gracie died were vague; anything that had occurred in the run up to her sister's body being discovered had been hijacked by the horror of the event. Her mother on her knees screaming, her dad with his hand on his heart, as if he might topple over and die too. Numerous police officers in the hallway and the kitchen. The blue flashing lights of their vehicles, quite unnecessary on their wide sweep of driveway, they filled the hallway with their cool tone. It reminded her of being at the bottom of a swimming pool, something she'd liked to do when the weather allowed, trying to see how long she could hold her breath, as she battled to stay submerged in her floral swimming hat and matching costume. Her auntie Nesta running in and grabbing her mother around the waist, the two women falling to the floor in the sitting room, a jumble of arms and legs and then her aunt's screams matching those of her mother. Her sweet cousin Darius sitting on the end of her bed. They'd sat in silence as the house grew dark and no one came upstairs to offer them food or drink or check in. It felt like everyone for themselves and about as scary.

Verity liked the sudden warmth that coated her skin, it felt like, like sunshine! She opened her eyes, fighting to take a steady breath… and there she was in her parents' carefully tended back garden, laying on a tartan blanket in her cut-offs and vest. It was a miracle, it was magic! Beautiful, beautiful magic because right there next to her, in a denim bikini, was her stunning big sister, *Gracie!* Reaching out, she ran her fingertips over her sister's arm, confirming she was real.

'You trying to tickle me?'

Verity shook her head, stunned! How was this possible? Aware then of her long hair, forgetting how it had felt, the swish of locks around her face, the weight of it on her shoulders. She looked down at her striped T-shirt, her arms skinny, chest only starting to bud.

Gracie's skin was covered in freckles that gave her a burnished hue. Her auburn hair caught the sunlight, and her pale blue eyes were laughing. She looked happy, so happy, as she propped her head on her hand, her elbow planted on the blanket.

'You look really pretty.' It was the truth. Her voice riven with emotion. Gracie was striking and lovely, with a youthful roundness to her face and limbs. A young woman with the whole wide world at her feet. A million miles away from that rotten photo.

'Why are you being so nice to me?'

'I'm always nice to you!'

'No you're not, you snitch on me!' Gracie made out to jab her in the ribs.

'When did I snitch on you?' She had entirely forgotten if she had.

'When I took the gin from the sideboard that Mum'd bought for Christmas, you told them it was me.'

So she had! This memory wrapped now in deep regret.

'Well who else was it going to be?' she laughed, and Gracie laughed too. The loveliest sound. 'What are you doing tonight, any plans?' It was the closest she could get to discussing her sister's movements, aware of Chen's warning that any mention of what was to happen would be disastrous and their time would end. She was not about to let this incredible opportunity slip through her fingers.

'I'm going to a party, actually!' Her sister lay on her front and beat her feet on the blanket, excitement and energy making her limbs jump. 'But don't tell Mum and Dad; it's a secret.'

'Can I come with you?' If there was the slightest chance that she might be able to tag along, stick to her sister's side, stop her meeting the most terrible fate, but, of course, that was impossible. Everything had already happened. This was no more than VR, a snapshot, at least that was how she tried to explain it to herself.

'No, you dork, you can't. It's not your kind of party. Maybe in a few years.'

'Who're you going with?'

'Well aren't you full of questions!' Gracie leaned forward, held her hair to one side, and whispered conspiratorially, 'If you must know, I'm going with my boyfriend.'

'You haven't got a boyfriend!' This was news.

'I have, actually, but he's a secret too. And don't tell a soul, but I'm only going to the party to show my face and then I'm meeting him and we're going to hang out in his car, put some music on. Have a wee drinkie! God, I'm so into him!'

'He's got a car?'

'Even better than that, he's got a truck.' Gracie widened her eyes as if this was currency.

'Do you love him, Gracie?' she asked softly.

Her sister nodded, her tone sincere, 'And he loves me.'

'Are you shagging?'

Gracie let out a raucous howl, 'God, that is the funniest thing in the world, hearing you say the word shagging!'

'I'm fourteen, not a baby!'

'You're our baby, V, always will be.'

'So, *are* you?' Verity wanted the detail.

'Aye. It's like a drug! I'm totally addicted, can't get enough of him.' She threw her head back and took a deep breath.

'So who is it?'

'Can't say.' Gracie shook her head.

'You can tell me. I want to know!' She felt the bloom of tears at the back of her throat. 'Is it, is it Dale McCurdy?' She hated the feel of his name in her mouth.

Gracie sprayed her laughter, 'Dale McCurdy! Urgh! Jesus Christ!' she made out to retch. 'You've giein me the boak! Why would you think that? *Dale McCurdy*? He's a complete waste of space! Dale McCurdy, of all people*?'* – she laughed again – 'Are you kidding? Do I not have standards?'

'So who is it then?' Verity sat up and stared at her darling sister. 'I promise not to tell anyone.'

Gracie sat up too and toyed with a chain around her neck. She bit her lip as if keen to share the information, in the way you did when you were excited, in love and seventeen. Her beautiful, beautiful sister, *only seventeen...*

'If you say a word to anybody, I'll never speak to you again.' Her eyes glinted with seriousness.

'Cross my heart.' Verity made the sign.

'It's Jon.'

'Jon?' She thought hard, unable to think of a single Jon. There was no Jon on the school bus, no Jon in her sister's friendship group, not a single Jon came to mind. 'Jon who?'

It was then that her sister leaned close and, with a blush to her face and neck, whispered into Verity's ear, 'Jon Morton.'

'But,' pulling away she stared at her sister. 'Mr Morton, Dad's friend?'

'He's hardly Dad's friend, but yeah, him.'

'But,' again words failed her. 'He's *old!* He's married!' Verity pictured the wealthy farmer whose kids were in the year below her at school.

'Age is just a number, V, and, as for married, he won't be for much longer. He's going to leave her, for me. Well, actually, he's going to ask her to leave. You'll be able to come and visit me up at the big house, I'll make you a cuppa tea. I've already told him I'll need to redecorate. Can't be living with another woman's wallpaper.'

It was as sad as it was ironic that her sister naively announced she couldn't live with the woman's wallpaper but was happy to live with her husband. It was new information, terrible and revealing new information! *Jon Morton!* A man who stood to lose a lot if his affair with his young neighbour were to be made public and if Gracie had told her …

Verity didn't know what to do, what to say! But the pressure to do something was almost overwhelming.

'Gracie…' Verity took her sister's hands into her own. 'I, I don't think seeing him is a good idea. He's married! You'd be better off with someone your own age!'

'Two things. First, we're in love, and second, as if I'd take advice from you!'

'Please, Gracie, please.' It was as close as she could come to begging, and then it occurred to her, the time was running out anyway, what if there were the slightest chance… Verity took a deep breath and spoke with urgency. 'I love you, I love you so much, don't go to the party tonight, please, Gracie! Don't g—'

It felt as if she were being flung backwards with force. Her spine hit the sofa and she found herself back in the lounge of the house she shared with Patrick. Dottie barked in the kitchen before she came trotting in. Winded, it took Verity a minute, as she moved onto all fours, head hanging down, trying to catch her breath.

'Jesus! Oh, Jesus!'

Jon Morton. The question now was what was she to do with the information?

Reaching for her phone, she fired a text off to her Dad. The man who had inadvertently given her a clue – *a place where everyone pulled together to face whatever came their way, looking after each other, like family, protecting their own.*

YOU AWAKE?

He called her almost instantly, as she'd hoped he might.

'I don't require half as much sleep as I used to, Hen, everything okay?' She hated the note of concern in his voice. 'Not like you to call so late on a Saturday night!'

'Dad, this is going to sound very odd.' She closed her eyes, it made it easier somehow. 'Are you sitting down?'

'I am now,' he whispered. 'You're scaring me, Verity.'

She decided to cut to the chase. 'This is going to sound mad, but I think I know who killed Gracie, and why.'

'Goodness me,' he breathed heavily down the line, 'I… I don't know what to say, tell me!'

'I believe she was having an affair with Jon Morton. A man who had a lot to lose if that ever got out.'

'Jon Morton…' He spoke the name quite calmly, a surprise in itself. 'Now that's a very strange thing.'

'How so, Dad?'

'Your mother said something very similar just before she died. I assumed it was the morphine talking. She wasn't making a lot of sense. God love her. *Jon Morton?'*

'Yes, old enough and clever enough to let a waste of space like Dale McCurdy fall under suspicion. But I'm sure it was him, Dad. Did Mum say anything else?'

'Ah, my beloved wife, I asked her how she knew, I mean it sounded so far-fetched, and she said that, she said that,' his voice broke then, giving way to tears, 'she said Gracie had told her.'

'Oh, Dad!' Verity put her hand over her eyes and matched him tear for tear. 'Poor Gracie!'

'Aye, poor, poor Gracie.' He echoed. 'I don't know what to make of it, Verity, but we'll not let it drop. We'll go back to the police. I still have friends on the force. The Mortons are still up at the big house. If it's him, Verity, I swear to God, I'll—'

'Dad, you need to keep calm, and we need to let the powers that be do their job. But we'll face it together, whatever comes next, we'll muddle through.'

'Aye, we'll muddle through.' He sniffed. 'But, how, Verity, how did you come to know this?'

'Erm,' she stroked Dottie's back and took a deep breath. 'That's the thing, Dad, Gracie told me too...'

Chapter Six - Benjamin Stokes-Rattigan

Aged 30

Poole, Dorset

Benjamin Stokes-Rattigan was in a state of shock. Standing now in the shower, he let the jets of hot water hit his skin, which was pleasant and uncomfortable all at once. Reluctant to step out of the cubicle, he took his time, knowing, once he did, the day would begin in earnest, events would flow, timings would be adhered to and he'd be swept along by the tide, part of the spectacle.

He wasn't ready, knew he'd never be ready, not really.

'Don't take forever, Benjamin, the cars will be here in an hour!'

'You think I don't know that, Marcus!' he barked, instantly regretting his tone. It wasn't Marcus' fault. His younger brother, like him, was only doing his best to keep control of this surreal situation, trying to get through.

It was an odd time, the period between his father dying and today, the funeral. Fourteen days during which he had taken trips down memory lane, picturing childhood holidays where they'd played in the sand or his dad threw him high in the swimming pool, only to catch him again. The man ruffling his hair with affection and wrapping him in a warm hug.

Lovely though these recollections were, he had no idea where they had come from as, whoever these memories belonged to, they certainly weren't his! Throughout his youth there had been numerous holidays to exclusive islands in warm places, ski trips where roaring fires awaited them after a day on the slopes, weeks spent on yachts in the BVI, and they'd eaten in *Michelin* starred restaurants the way others ordered chicken nuggets and went large for an extra couple of quid. Hugh Stokes-Rattigan was a man whose idea of casual dining was to loosen his tie. During all of these jaunts, and always with a nanny or assistant in tow, his father was strangely absent. Often present physically, but usually with a phone pressed to his ear or a laptop within tip-tapping distance or he'd be having a business discussion with a never seen before associate who would join them at the table and garner all of his attention.

In the days since the man's death, Benjamin had watched a stream of visitors press the main gate for entry and make their way along the gravel path with flowers for Allegra and casseroles, of all things. It made him smile, as if his father's wife would eat casserole made in a stranger's kitchen. She wouldn't. Unless those casseroles were vegan, macrobiotic and organic, and she'd had a chance to scrupulously inspect their kitchen and hygiene practices, which he very much doubted.

Allegra was a mystery to him. His stepmother of sorts and the second woman to hold the title in ten years, but at only six years older than him it was hard to view her as anything other than his father's partner, definitely not motherly. Besides, he already had a mother, and she was wonderful.

Allegra was solely responsible for influencing his father's decision to have a hair transplant, which had been very successful. Tooth veneers, which were dazzling. To upgrade his designer wardrobe, which was a bit hit and miss, Benjamin felt that cowboy boots on any man not a cowboy was a bit iffy. And of course his decision to purchase an Arancio Borealis coloured Lambo Huracan, which had proved to be a mistake, a big one, as it was now in three pieces, having wrapped itself around a sturdy oak tree on a tight bend.

Hence, the funeral.

In the aftermath of the accident, the house had felt busier than usual, as the police (emergency service, not the group), the local vicar, a funeral director, florists, a team from the bank and many of his father's employees all at various times, took seats in the library or study, wearing similar solemn, grey-faced expressions. Allegra and Marcus had dealt with the vicar and bank; everyone else, he had greeted.

It seemed comical, a bit of a farce, as he shook hands with the men and women who only viewed him as Hugh's son, a pretender, as he took his father's chair behind the big desk, feeling horribly uncomfortable. Truth was he was inclined to agree with them, it all felt like pretending.

This was not a feeling new to Benjamin, who, at the age of eighteen – with a weighty gold watch on his wrist, gifted to him by his dad along with the words, *'you're a man now'* – hadn't felt like a man. Instead he'd felt like an eighteen-year-old with a very fancy watch, but not a clue about life or how to live it.

Again at twenty-one – having signed on the dotted line, as his father proclaimed, '*You're a director now'* – he hadn't felt like a director. He'd felt like a twenty-one-year-old with a title, and a very fancy three-year-old watch, who still didn't have the first clue about life or how to live it.

Most of the staff he greeted wanted to offer him reassurance that his father's business interests could be left safely in their care during this most unfortunate period of transition.

The car dealerships.

Yacht chandlery.

Boat sheds.

Hotels.

Office complex.

Estate Agency.

…and gyms.

What they were *actually* asking, and what they *really* wanted to know, was what was going to happen next? Were their jobs safe? Who was taking over? How would it all work?

He wished he had the answers.

His response had been pretty much the same for all parties. 'Thank you for your condolences. We'll do our best to get through this and then work on the detail when things have settled down…'

Even he wasn't sure what this word salad meant, but noted how most went away with a spring in their step and dropped shoulders indicating a lack of tension, which was good.

'My job is to keep the ship steady.' His father said this a lot.

Benjamin, unfortunately, had always had a tendency towards sea sickness, especially on choppy water.

He had, as the oldest child, been tasked with delivering his father's eulogy. A matter that weighed most heavily on his gym-honed shoulders which showed no sign of dropping any time soon. He'd sat at the dining room table with a leather-bound notebook open and his trusty *Mont Blanc* in his hand, tapping the weighty writing instrument on the blank page, hoping words might fall from the nib.

They didn't.

He resorted to *Google* and read how others had paid homage to their fathers in their darkest hours. One or two missives seemed eloquent and heartfelt. He cut and pasted the text onto his phone, deciding to edit the words and rework them to fit the way he felt about his father.

It was only after he'd scratched through the bits that didn't apply and blanked out anything too schmalzy that he abandoned this method too.

~~'I really, really loved my Dad. He was my hero! Always there for me, he was my best friend, my guardian angel even in life!~~ He loved cricket. ~~My dad was my biggest cheerleader, I will be forever thankful for his guidance. He was my rock.~~'

'How's the urology going?' Allegra had asked only a couple of days ago. His stepmother was, as he'd heard his father once cruelly describe her, untroubled by the weight of intellect.

'Umm.' Ordinarily he'd have made a straight-faced comment about the amount of study required, and how it was the male genitourinary tract, with fiddly details of the kidneys, bladder, and prostate that were proving most taxing. But he didn't, not when they were in this sticky limbo between death and funeral. Emotions were running high, and Allegra's mascara looked permanently smudged, suggesting tears or excessive laughter, he wasn't sure which. 'Good, yeah, good.' Felt safer.

The fact that he was now only an hour or so away from having to stand in front of the great and good of his father's circle and every distant relative and acquaintance this side of Bath, to deliver a speech about the man himself, was nothing short of terrifying.

'Benjamin, cars will be here in about an hour!'

'Yep, thanks,' he called out to Allegra. He was never late, yet today everyone seemed to think he might rock up when it suited him, missing the grand entrance entirely or, worse still, arriving as everyone was leaving.

Now wouldn't that be terrible.

Yes, Benjamin was in a state of shock. Not because of his father's untimely demise, although, yes, that too, but more because of a very peculiar visit that had occurred five days ago.

'There's a bloke in Dad's study.' Marcus had spoken, mouth full of bagel, as Benjamin entered the kitchen that morning in search of coffee.

'Who is it?'

'Dunno!' his brother shrugged.

'Well, is he here to fix something, deliver something, talk to someone?' The lack of detail was irritating.

'Talk to you.' Marcus clicked his fingers, as if only just remembering, and took another large bite of bagel. 'He said he was here to talk to you.'

'Bloody hell, I'm supposed to be meeting Dan.' His friend, and the pickleball court, would just have to wait.

Opening the study door, he saw the back of the man, suited, booted and staring at his father's impressive portrait which hung over the fireplace.

'That's some painting.' He whistled, turning to smile at Benjamin.

'Yes, a terrible loss. Erm, forgive me, but do you have an appointment, I didn't catch your name?' He did his best to make the necessary enquiries without appearing rude.

'That's because I haven't given anyone my name yet!' the man laughed. 'My name is Chen.'

'Chen-?'

'Just Chen!' he laughed.

'I see, well, *Just Chen,* thank you so much for stopping by, how can I help you?' The grandfather clock ticked loudly, a reminder that time was passing, and Dan would be warming up.

'Might we sit down?' Chen nodded towards the desk and the wide leather chairs on either side.

'Sure, although I don't have too much time, I'm already late for—'

'Daniel won't mind waiting,' Chen spoke, as he sat in front of the desk.

'You know Daniel?' It was curious, who was this guy?

'I know everyone!' Chen laughed and Benjamin laughed too, taking his father's seat behind the desk.

'Yes, it's a small place. What can I do for you, Chen?' he coughed to clear the awkwardness from his throat.

'It's more a question of what I can do for you.'

'Oh! I see.' He sat back in the chair, as the penny dropped. This kind of tactic wasn't unheard of, yet it was still a shock that someone might consider this a good time to shoot their shot. When you had plenty of money, you were often a magnet for those with a great idea, a brilliant scheme, a brand-new product, a revolutionary service, or the best X, Y or Z you have *ever* tasted! This guy, it seemed, was no more than a chancer who had managed to get into the house, and now Benjamin needed to figure out how to get him out of the house with the minimum amount of fuss.

He placed his phone on the desktop, knowing a quick button press would summon the gardener who was somewhere on the grounds. Ignacio was ex special forces, as skilled with his fists and a carefully concealed baton as he was with a pair of secateurs.

'I fear you've had a wasted journey, Chen, but I would like to thank you for taking the time out to—'

'You won't need to call Ignacio.' Chen joined his hands and folded them into his lap. 'I mean you no harm.'

'What the hell is going on here?' Benjamin sat forward in the chair with a growing sense of alarm. 'You've clearly been studying me, studying us, what is it you want?' His patience was waning.

'I want to tell you something, it won't take long, but I think it might help you, Benjamin.'

'And how much is this "help" going to cost me?' he drew inverted commas in the air.

'It's free, actually.' Chen smiled.

'Free? So what's in it for you?'

'It's my job.' The man clicked his tongue on the roof of his mouth.

'Okay, let's hear it.' He sighed, joining his hands on the desktop, still with one eye on the clock. 'You've got five minutes, tops.'

The man spoke slowly, his tone calming and hypnotic.

'What I am going to tell you will sound implausible, ridiculous even, but trust me when I tell you that I have never and will never tell you a lie…'

Chen's visit had been comical. Benjamin, having ushered him out of the door, had laughed and laughed, managing to put the words of the charlatan out of his mind by the time he finally made it to pickleball, where he and Daniel had thrashed it out on the court.

It was the next night, Saturday, while Allegra was in her room, Marcus was out with the lads, and Ignacio was in his cottage by the main gate, that Benjamin found himself sitting in the very chair Chen had occupied at a little before eleven p.m.

He laughed to himself, as he stared at the imposing portrait of his father, took a slug of the old man's brandy in a cut glass tumbler and closed his eyes.

'What *are* you doing, Benjamin?' he'd laughed, wondering if he might work this moment of madness into the bloody eulogy – maybe mentioning how grief had taken him on a trip that had resulted in him sitting in the chair of his father's study, believing he might be about to communicate with the dead. If nothing else, he figured it would lighten the mood, guarantee a laugh.

'What are you smirking at?'

Benjamin took a sharp intake of breath. It wasn't possible, couldn't be possible, but there he was! His father! Sitting in the big chair opposite him on the other side of the desk. It came back to him then, all of it, this moment – about four months ago, he'd popped in to get some paperwork signed, Hugh had just arrived back from a trip to Zurich.

'N... nothing, Dad! I, I,'

'Spit it out!'

He'd almost forgotten how he stuttered in his father's presence. What did he want to say? What was important? He tried to recall how long Chen had said he'd be given, was it ten minutes? He knew it wasn't long. The time pressure only added to his nerves. It was bizarre seeing the man alive, whole and unblemished and yet curiously he felt very little, not like if his lovely mum were to pass and he got to see her again. A lump formed in his throat at no more than the prospect. He loved her dearly and she loved him, it was a wonderful and comforting thing, that knowledge.

'Did, did you love my mum?'

'Good Lord! Did I love your mother, where on earth has that come from?' Hugh asked with a confused expression. The Stokes-Rattigans didn't do emotion. Never had. 'I suppose so. But you know what they say, Benjamin, all good things come to an end.'

'They also say, all good things come to those who wait. Maybe if you'd waited until she was better, finished her treatment, you might have been given the biggest reward of all, you might even have been happy.'

He knew he would never have found the confidence to speak so plainly if his father were not dead and this were not a once in a lifetime opportunity. His father spoke plainly.

'Possibly, but I think happiness is overrated.'

'You do?' there was nothing left his father could say that would shock him, but this came close.

'Yes. People think it's everything, but happiness is only one emotion. Why are we all so obsessed with it?'

'B… because it feels nice?'

'Poppycock! So does a warm bath, a cold G & T, hitting a hole in one in front of the club chairman, and getting a seat on the train, yet they can't become the driving force of life! It's a ridiculous notion! Power feels nice. Winning feels nice. Success feels nice!'

'And they make you happy?' he pushed.

'Not always. For me it's about getting right on to the next thing, facing the next challenge, that makes me feel good. Keeping busy!'

'Maybe, contentment is the answer?' Benjamin spoke softly.

'Good lord! Contentment is for goldfish and simpletons! You see them, don't you? Average Joes walking around in tracksuits, hand in hand in revolting displays of sentimentality, only worrying about what beige thing to have for supper and looking forward to watching something on the telly! Give me strength! Such small, small lives.'

'It must be exhausting, Dad, always getting right on to the next thing. Don't you ever want to rest?'

'I'll rest when I'm dead.' His father winked. 'I have responsibilities, need to keep the ship steady.'

'I've never really known what that means,' he levelled.

His father let out a nasal snort of irritation, 'It means I have to have a hand on the tiller at all times! Means I need to keep an eye on all aspects of our business interests to make sure they don't all go tits up and we lose the bloody lot!' He wiped the spittle from the corner of his mouth. 'It means that every little thing needs my approval, from the colour of the walls in this study to where to invest next, or the brand of bloody fabric softener we use on the towels in the gym. Standards, Benjamin!'

'Jesus!' it was a scary insight into just how tightly his dad gripped that tiller.

'Not sure what he's got to do with it, but can you try and be a bit less flippant, what's got into you? You sound like your mother!'

'I think if, if I sound like Mum it's a good thing.' he pictured his lovely mum.

His father stared, a slight twitch below his left eye.

'I sometimes wonder if you're made of the right stuff, Benjamin.'

'Do you know, Dad.' He stood, aware that, if he left the room, he'd lose any remaining time and in that moment caring less. 'I sometimes wonder that too.'

'And now what, are you flouncing off to lick your wounds?'

He stared at his dad, seeing the glint of cruelty in his eye, the thin-lipped disapproval that dripped from his mouth.

'Do you… do you love *me*, Dad? Because you've never made it clear, never said it.' He gripped the back of the chair.

'What in Christ's name has got into you? You must be nearly thirty, bit late for wanting a cuddle from daddy!'

'I am thirty,' he corrected.

Hugh continued unabashed.

'Do you think my father ever told me he loved me, do you think he hugged me and brought me warm milk and cookies, read me a bedtime bloody story?'

'I'm guessing not.'

'You'd guess right, and it made me the man I am!' Hugh banged his hand on the desk.

It saddened him not to receive a response.

'You haven't answered my question, Dad, do you love me?'

Hugh looked down at the desk and took a moment, his discomfort evident. And it spoke volumes. It saddened him, that his father had not experienced the warm and comforting knowledge that Benjamin shared with his mother, would never know what it felt like to love your child and be loved in return.

'I think it's very easy, Dad, to say I do, I love you, I love you! It takes seconds, and would, I think, make all the difference.'

Benjamin turned to leave the room, and, in the same second, shuddered, finding himself once more alone at the desk with his brandy.

'What the hell!' He took slow breaths, staring at the painting of the old man above the mantelpiece. 'What the actual hell!'

So yes, Benjamin Stokes-Rattigan was in shock, and it wasn't solely down to the fact that his father had died, but more what had occurred in the study, when he'd been gifted time by Chen. Stepping from the shower, he dried himself slowly and wiped the steam from the mirror, staring at the face looking back at him.

'I guess that's the question, are you made of the right stuff?' he asked, saddened, again not to receive a response.

The church was, as he'd expected, busy. His mother took a seat towards the back of the room. She stood out to him, the woman who loved him unconditionally. It was surreal, hearing the accolades listed of the man who was his father, listening to the stirring music while the mahogany and brass coffin bedecked in lilies sat on a trestle by the alter, closest to God.

'...and now his son, Benjamin.'

He almost missed his cue, before standing and walking briskly to the shiny brass lectern, still quite unsure of what to say, where to start.

'Thank you all for coming here today.' His voice rang out. It threw him a little. 'I know it would mean a lot to my father to see this service so well attended. What can I say about Hugh Stokes-Rattigan? He was a man who, who loved cricket.' He paused. 'A man who believed happiness was overrated and that contentment is for goldfish and simpletons.' He looked out over the congregation whose expressions were mostly perplexed. 'He was married to my mother for a while, his first wife. She's a remarkable woman, my mum. She lives quietly and kindly in a cottage along the coast. My father left her when she was fighting breast cancer. I'm sure he loved her in his own way, but all good things come to an end, right?' There was the faint ripple of awkward laughter that echoed up to the rafters.

'I've come to the conclusion over the last couple of weeks that, actually, *I'm* a simpleton.' This time, as he spoke with tears sheeting his face and all eyes on him, the room was very quiet, gripped by the sincerity of his words, 'I'm not my father. I want to walk around in a tracksuit and worry about what to have for supper. I want to look forward to watching something on the telly. I want to figure out life and how to live it. I want not to feel like an imposter. I don't want to keep the ship steady, I want to dive into the water and swim!' His head fell forward, as his sadness poured from him, and he wiped away his tears with the palm of his hand. 'I'd like to end by saying, that's my advice to you all, especially you, Marcus.' He held his brother's gaze, 'just dive into the water, and swim.'

It was as he walked from behind the brass lectern that Marcus shook his head, and mouthed, 'Dickhead!'

The air outside the church was fresh, the sky blue, and the sun did its best to make its presence felt.

Benjamin looked back at the solid doors of the church where *He Who Would Valiant Be* was being sung with vigour.

'You might be right, Marcus, but I'm a dickhead who is free! I'm bloody free!'

Loosening his tie, he ran then, down to the beach, towards the sea.

He began to hum the tune of *Message in a Bottle*, by The Police (the group, not the emergency service) – knowing he was done with being lonely and was not about to risk *his* life falling into despair.

'Thank you, Chen!' he called, as he kicked of his well-polished shoes, peeled off his cashmere socks, and prepared to dive in…

'Thank you!'

Chapter Seven - Mikey Charles Frewin

Aged 47

Thornton, Liverpool

'Can I get you anything before I head off?' Mikey asked from the bedroom door, wary of disturbing the lump in the middle of their bed, yet equally fearful of abandoning her at this time. He always knew it was going to be a difficult few days, and it was.

'No.'

He had to listen hard to make out her response, no more than a thin whisper from a throat riven with sadness, as if every word that left her mouth had to travel over broken glass.

'I thought you might, might want a cup of tea, or —'

'No.' Her voice a little firmer now, and he got the message.

'Do you want me to open the window, Gemma?' The room was, he felt, a little stuffy, the air stagnant, less than fragrant, as particles of misery gathered in the corners and settled on the windowsill and the top of the white IKEA chest of drawers that sat by the door.

'Please, Mikey, just...'

She shifted in the bed, like a sea creature breaching the surface, taking air, and disappearing again beneath the duvet, the arc of her waning hip the only recognisable outline.

'Okay,' he took a step into the hallway, 'but if you need anything. I'll keep my phone on all day...' he let this trail and pulled the door almost closed, wanting not to miss it if she called out, and wanting her to hear the sound of life, the chatter on the TV, the click and whistle of the kettle. Him, running taps, flushing the loo. He figured it was important, a reminder that life went on.

Whether you wanted it to or not.

Turning on the narrow strip of landing, he trod the stairs slowly, trying not to let his eyes stray to the box room that had become the spare room when they'd saved enough money to put a bed in it, then Aaron's room when he'd arrived. One day, he guessed, it might return to a spare room, but not yet, no time soon.

Just the thought of tidying away his things, more than he could stand.

Friday morning, and the atmosphere in their two-up two-down in Thornton, Liverpool, was fraught. It was the anniversary. One year. It seemed to have passed quickly now it arrived, yet also could have been a decade or more if you looked at how Mikey's face had aged, etched by grief and a lack of restorative sleep, Gemma's too, not that he'd be cruel enough to ever mention it.

He would say they'd rallied a little this summer. Some days were even pleasant. Not happy, but bearable. His sister, Pat, and the kids had come over for a barbecue one time and Gemma's brother, Ian, and his wife popped in on the way back from town. They'd drank a beer or two in the garden, Gemma put crisps in bowls and rummaged in the freezer for ice cream. It was easier to forget somehow when they were in company. Not entirely, never that, but having a conversation, hearing news, sharing a laugh, reminiscing, it all helped dilute the sticky syrup of loss that ran sluggishly through their veins. Helped them paint on a mask, to present like they were coping.

When it happened. Mikey thought he'd never laugh or feel steady again, expecting to fall flat on his face every time he took a step. He thought Gemma would never stop sobbing, thought they were finished because staring at a face that mirrored your own, tear for tear, horror for horror, was almost more than either of them could stand. They found themselves plunged into an icy pool of grief with such speed and ferocity they didn't have time to take a breath before it was over their heads. In that icy pool they bobbed, cold and adrift in the darkness, searching for something to cling to, their cries of help echoing into the abyss.

They came close to going their separate ways. She might even have packed a bag, spoken about going to her mum's, and honestly? He'd have let her, without the strength to lift a hand, raise an objection, or form a coherent counter argument. He couldn't recall now why she had stayed, but was very glad she did.

He loved her. Gemma, his childhood sweetheart.

Aaron's mum.

She was the only other person on the planet who felt the same way about Aaron, someone who not only shared so many vital memories of their son, but also the only other person on the planet who knew what he was going through.

It wasn't solely the anniversary of his death that was a marker, a dip, but also Aaron's birthday was approaching, a reminder that he was going to forever be twenty-four. His birthday just a week after they'd lost him. Christmas, Mother's Day, Father's Day, Mikey's birthday, Gemma's birthday, the day Pat's daughter, Amy, got married, so many times when there was an Aaron shaped gap in a photograph, a chair without him sitting on it, his quip missing from the banter. God, he missed him! Missed him with a pain that was physical, like there was something sticking in his chest. A wound that he didn't want to heal – not ever – as every minute of every day it reminded him of his boy.

He figured it was a price worth paying and would pay it gladly for a thousand lifetimes, just for the privilege of being Aaron's dad for twenty-four years.

The lads at work had stopped mentioning Aaron. Life moved on, and he understood. It was both a sadness and a relief, as each mention of him, every well-intentioned enquiry raised the image of his son on that morning. His face almost grey. Lips blue. Eyes open. The weird tilt to his neck and the cool touch to his alabaster skin. Mikey knew he'd never get over it, not ever. It was the first thing he saw when he woke in the morning and the last thing he saw before he fell asleep.

Mikey was only thankful it was he who had found him and not Gemma, able to cover him up, warn her as best as he was able, while screaming in a high-pitched voice, that he didn't know he possessed, for her to dial 999.

'Now, Gem! Right now! Call the police! The, the ambulance! Do it now! Oh Jesus! Oh my God! My God!'

His panicked words carried urgency, but in his heart he knew there was little point in calling anyone.

Aaron had gone.

His lad, just twenty-four.

The coroner's report confirmed a cocktail of pills, most likely ingested intentionally despite a lack of note. Not that it mattered what they wrote in their report, as Mikey knew it was his fault.

The first days and weeks were strangely both the hardest and the easiest. Locked in a tormented loop of retrospection, he found himself repeating in his head. *This time last month we went to the pub for supper. This time two weeks ago he sat in the car with me, as I drove him to Georgia's house. This time last week he called his Nan, she was so chuffed to chat.* His thoughts tumbling and shifting as he tried to reconcile the fact that Aaron's life, his presence, his routine, and his future had just stopped. But also, it was a time when there were the most people around, a constant stream of loved ones bringing food, flowers, cards and warm, warm words of condolence to their door.

It was when that ebbed, and the drama faded, that Mikey felt as if he was being sucked into a black hole that had no beginning or end. A sorrow-filled tunnel in which he might tumble for eternity. He had been happy before the loss of his son, a happily married, family man. Content. All he had ever wanted.

For he and Gemma, their grief became a secret thing. They'd smile when in public and at night sit on the sofa in silence. Faces collapsed. Shoulders slumped, spines softened. Each staring at the wall. Lights off. The sounds of the street filtering through the window; calls, greetings, dog barks, music, even laughter, all of it as if Aaron had not gone and the world was just the same as it had been before. But it wasn't. They were changed, wounded, hollow, and all the colours of the world had faded to grey.

On occasion they'd howl. A visceral call of distress as pain left their bodies in audial form.

This morning, Mikey had to focus. Sinking down into the soft leather sofa that he was paying off monthly, he ran his hand over his face and closed his eyes briefly. He was tired, so tired. Sleep had been evasive for the last couple of weeks. He toyed with the idea of calling in sick and crawling into bed next to Gemma, but it was his dad's words that came to him now, 'Those bills aren't goin' to pay themselves, kidda!'

It was true, and the push he needed to get on site and start digging.

His phone pinged, a text from Gemma, this apparently easier than calling down the stairs.

CAN YOU COLLECT MY TBLETS FROM CHMIST?

'I'll grab them after work, love,' he called up towards their bedroom before grabbing his flask and leaving through their front door.

***

Mikey felt a little self-conscious as he stood in the queue for the pharmacy at the back of the chemist. The sweat of his day's labour clung to his old hoodie, and his trousers were spattered with mud. He spoke to the bloke standing next to him.

'Are you next, mate?' He didn't want to push in, queue jump. He was a man who liked order and manners.

'No, I'm waiting, already been seen, thanks. You go ahead.'

'Cheers.' Stepping forward, he smiled at Liz, the woman who worked in the pharmacy and whose mum lived in the next street over from he and Gemma. Liz had been in the year below them at school.

'Hiya, mate.'

'Alight, Liz. Come to collect the prescription for Gem.' He pushed the slip of paper across the counter.

'Be a minute, love.'

'No rush.'

He retook his place further back, next to a man who now smiled at him.

'It's Mikey, isn't it?'

'Who's askin'?' He eyed the fella who now smiled at him.

'My name is Chen, I've been looking for you.'

'Is that right?' He didn't know who the smiling idiot was but, whoever he was, Mikey was in no mood for a chat.

'I have something to say that will seem strange, but hear me out…'

He stared ahead, as Chen spouted the biggest load of bullshit he'd ever heard! He watched people approach the counter and hand over their slips of paper while Liz and the pharmacist ran around sorting bottles, sachets, blister packs and tubes into small paper bags. He listened intently to what the weirdo said, keeping his cool just, arms folded tightly across his broad chest, heart racing.

'Here we go, Mikey!' Liz called and waved the paper bag in his direction. Before he stepped forward to accept the antidepressants that made Gemma feel better, he turned briefly towards Chen and spoke softly.

'Fuck off and leave me alone! And if we weren't in the chemist's and these people weren't my neighbours, I'd knock your fucking head off your shoulders, d'ya hear me?'

'I hear you, Mikey, but I wanted to give you the chance. It's not your fault. It was never your fault!'

With anger now rising in his chest, he shoulder-barged past the bloke, taking the bag from Liz, before walking quickly to his van, where he sat in the driver's seat, his chest heaving.

Death had a strange effect on people, that much he did know, remembering the dozens of best friends who had sobbed on social media at the loss of Aaron, most of whom neither he nor Gemma had ever heard of. This man, however, with his granting of bloody wishes, took strangeness to a whole other level. He was glad of two things, first that he'd managed to control his anger, and second that it wasn't Gemma the bloke had cornered, knowing how it would had unnerved her, and, if that had happened, then, inside the chemist or not, Mikey wouldn't have hesitated to knock his head off.

As his pulse calmed and his breath found a more natural rhythm, he regretted barging into him. I mean, who was he? Someone in need of help probably, someone in need of something. It was, as he was trying to swallow his guilt, that the man walked from the chemist's.

Mikey got out of the van and walked towards him.

'Look, I'm sorry for losing it a bit in there.'

'I understand, it's a lot.' Chen was not going to pack it in, clearly.

'I don't want you to say anything more,' Mikey spoke softly, 'but I do want to apologise for barging you like that.'

'No need to—'

'Please, let me finish,' he held up his hand, 'I don't think you can have any idea how cruel and beautiful your words were. Cruel because it's the dream, isn't it, the one wish we all have, to get a bit more time with them. And beautiful because just the thought of it, to see my boy, to touch him, hold him, hear him… It would mean everything, and I would give the rest of my life, happily, willingly, for just a minute with him!' His voice shook. 'But please, think before you spread this garbage. Talk to someone, Chen, talk to someone who can help *you.'*

'I promise you, Mikey, that I have never and will never tell you a lie!'

Turning slowly, Mikey made his way back to the van. He pulled out of the car park without looking back.

***

It was Saturday night, and Gemma hadn't left their bed, just as he'd expected. He now sat on the sofa and, despite the tension in his bones and wishing he could ignore what the weirdo in the chemist had said, he found himself entirely seduced by the idea of fifteen minutes with his son. When would he choose? That was an easy question, the last time he'd seen him, exactly a year ago when Aaron had come home from the pub and Mikey had been watching the footy on TV. The last time he'd heard his son's voice, without any hint of what was about to happen. He'd been distracted by the match and, when Aaron popped his head into the lounge and mentioned he and Georgia had finished, Mikey had leapt out of his seat to shout at a disallowed goal, arms flailing, voice loud,

'Come on, Ref! You've got to be bloody joking!'

He had, over the last twelve months, replayed the phrase and the moment endlessly. By the time he'd settled back into his chair and the furore over the goal had calmed down on screen, his son had climbed the stairs and closed his bedroom door.

And that was the last time he saw him.

Alive.

He would give anything – *anything* – to do it differently, to try and rid himself of the nightmare. Not that it would change what he believed to be the unshakeable truth, that it was his fault.

Taking a deep breath, he closed his eyes and tipped his head back on the sofa. It was strange, the way his body almost instantly felt different, as if without the weight of grief his whole being was lighter and gone was the feeling that there was something sticking in his chest. He opened his eyes and the commentator on TV was yelling:

'He is, he's going for it! The ball's moving to the forwards. It's three yards out from goal in the middle of the six-yard box – there's a tussle, the blues are defending, but too little too late, it's over the line! And let me tell you, Anfield is making some noise!'

Mikey felt light-headed, high! It was unbelievable! Fantastic and unbelievable! A dream? Possibly, but it felt so real! He was back in the room, a year ago.

Five, four, three…

He stared at the lounge door, which was ajar, knowing the exact timing of his son's entrance, having re-lived it night and day, day and night. Was he really going to get to see his boy? He placed his wide palm over his mouth to stop himself from calling out to Gemma, torn between not wanting her to miss it but also recalling what Chen had said, *'If you leave the room, alert anyone or the person themselves as to what is happening, your time with them will end.'*

He couldn't take the risk.

'Oh, wait a minute, this doesn't look good, the ref's calling for VAR—'

Two... one...

'Hiya,' his son's voice. One word that made his knees weaken, as emotion roared in his chest.

Mikey stood, just as he had, but this time he grabbed the remote control and turned off the TV.

'Hi!' the word a strangled whisper.

'Just going to go straight up, Dad.' Aaron pointed up the stairs.

It was hard to move, to function, to breathe!

'No, come in, come in!' Gathering himself, he walked over and waited as his son looked first up the stairs and then at the lounge before making the decision to step into the room.

Mikey, shaking, wrapped him in a rare hug. Holding him close, he breathed in his aftershave, the faint essence of lager, and minty gum. They rarely touched each other in this way, but tonight, Aaron, who Mikey knew would ordinarily pull away, shrug himself loose, make a joke, allowed himself to be held.

Mikey never wanted to let him go, content to stand there forever, but knew enough to keep things as normal as he was able, wanting those full fifteen minutes.

'You alright, Dad?'

'Yeah, just, you know, it's been a long week. Sit down.' He sat at one end of the sofa and Aaron the other.

He took the chance to take in every detail of his appearance, replacing the image that lived in his mind of that grey complexion, the staring eyes. Aaron was fuller in the face than he'd remembered, his hair longer.

He was beautiful. His beautiful boy.

'A good night?' He tried to keep the enquiry light, to appear calm, as his stomach churned, his blood ran fast, and he had to bite his lip to prevent words of warning firing from his mouth,

'Don't do it, son!'

'Think of what it'd do to your Mam, to me!'

'You have a bright future, lad, the brightest!'

'We love you, Aaron, you'll never know how much we love you!'

'Not really.' His son paused. 'Georgia dumped me—'

'Sorry to hear that,' Mikey spoke softly. 'Your mum finished with me once, you know.'

'Did she?'

'Yeah,' Mikey laughed, 'I was devastated!'

'What happened?' Aaron leaned forward. It took all of Mikey's strength not to grip his hands, look him in the eye and beg him to stay.

'It was a long time ago. I think she got cold feet. We were very young, about your age, and some of her mates were moving away, heading off to college or whatever, and I think she was worried about getting left behind. Settling.'

'But she settled for you in the end?'

'No, Aaron, that's the thing, everyone was saying, *there's plenty more fish in the sea,* as if I should have gone fishing for a new bird, but, instead, I chose her, and she chose me. Settling would have been the biggest mistake, always is. We chose each other.'

'And you lived happy ever after!'

'Again, no, lad!'

His son laughed, and it was wonderful to hear, so very wonderful!

'Life's difficult and relationships aren't easy, but we carry on choosing each other every day and we face whatever comes together. It's hard to accept when you're young, but the truth is most days are boring, tiring, and it's the small things she does that make me laugh or make me comfortable or make me happy that mean I want to get up in the morning and want to get home to her at night. I'll always work as hard as I can for you both. I'll always love you both to the bloody moon and back. You two are me world, me whole world!'

He couldn't help the tears that fell, no longer ashamed or embarrassed by the display, in the way he had once been, because crying was now, unfortunately, second nature to him.

'So you think Georgia might take me back?'

Mikey gripped his son's arm and looked him in the eye. 'She might, but the question is, do you want to put your happiness in the pocket of someone who has dumped you?

You need to understand her reasons and then make a decision.'

His son nodded.

'It's been a shite week, Dad. I, I messed up at work.' Aaron folded his hands, as his knee jumped with nervous energy.

He did not know this!

'You did? How?'

'Didn't connect the alternator properly on the boss's wife's car. She broke down in the Mersey Tunnel. He's mad as hell.'

'He'll calm down, lad. We all make mistakes. Talk to him, tell him you know you messed up, he'll respect that, and I know that you won't do it again.'

'I bloody won't!' Aaron exhaled a long, slow release. 'I'm tired, Dad.'

Mikey watched him stand, with fear in his chest that made his limbs shake.

'Aaron—'

'Wha?' his son asked, one hand on the door.

'It will all be okay. We love you, your mum and I, we love you so much.'

'You had a bevvy or two, Dad?'

'Not yet!' He felt the moments slipping away, and his heart squeezed in his chest. 'See you in the morning, Dad'

'Yep.' His voice cracked and he swallowed, forcing the lie from his lips. 'See you in the morning, love.'

***

Mikey woke in his bed with the curtains open and sunlight filling the room. He was relieved to see that Gemma was already up. This promised a better day than yesterday. Instantly he noticed the bedroom was clean, vacuumed, fresher than it had felt in recent times.

Treading the stairs, he heard the unfamiliar sound of music coming from the radio in the kitchen. The upbeat sound of pop fracturing the air that was usually silent and weighted. It was at once jarring and uplifting to be reminded of something he had once taken for granted, in the house that had grown as quiet as it was dark.

'Here he is! Rip van Winkle! What time d'you call this?' Gemma plonked a cup of tea on the countertop in front of him and kissed his cheek.

'Thanks.' He studied her, his wife who had washed and brushed her hair, was dressed and smiling, and moved with speed and ease of movement around their little kitchen. Gone was the stilted hesitance to her limbs as if every action caused her physical pain. Gone were the dark shadows of loss that lived beneath her eyes.

'What you staring at?' she fired, biting into thickly buttered toast and speaking with her mouth full.

'You.' He smiled. 'You look lovely.'

'Flippin' 'eck, what are you after?' she blushed. 'What time did you come up last night?'

Mikey sipped the tea. It tasted good. 'Not sure.'

'Recovered then from your upset over the footy?'

Placing the mug on the surface, he gripped the counter to keep himself upright. It was then he heard the sound of the TV in the lounge and the voice of commentary,

'He is – he's going for it! The ball's moving to the forwards. It's three yards out from goal in the middle of the six-yard box – there's a tussle, the blues are defending, but too little too late, it's over the line! And let me tell you, Anfield is making some noise! Oh, wait a minute, this doesn't look good, the ref's calling for VAR!'

Rising slowly, he walked along the hallway, listening intently, hardly daring to step into the lounge. Then he heard it, the sweet, sweet unmistakable sound of Aaron, his boy.

'Come on, Ref! You've got to be bloody joking!'

Mikey stood in the doorway, as his son jumped up, arms flailing, as he watched the match on catch up.

'You seen this, Dad?' he pointed at the TV screen with the remote control. Mikey fell against the wall, his tears beating a steady path down his stubbled face, his breath coming in huge gasps between sobs. It was a miracle, a second chance, it was… he couldn't find the words. That man, Chen, he'd shoulder barged him, when what he wanted to do was find him, hug him, thank him, ask him to explain!

'Jesus, Dad! It's only a goal!'

'Aaron!' Scrambling to his knees, he took his son into his arms and cried as he held him close. 'I had the most terrible nightmare, the worst.'

His son shrugged himself free and sat back down on the sofa.

'Give over! Have you had a bash to the head?'

'I might have,' he laughed, swiping at the tears that fell, 'I just might have.'

'Is Georgia coming for lunch, love?' Gemma asked from the doorway.

'Nah, we've broken up.'

'Ah, that's a shame, I like her. It's true what they say though, Aaron, there's plenty more fish in the sea!'

'So I've heard.'

Aaron smiled at his dad, and Mikey knew he would never be more thankful, for this moment, for *every* moment he got to spend with his boy.

His beautiful boy.

Mikey didn't want to let him out of his sight but took a moment to walk out into the back yard, his words he let fly high, 'I reckon you must have been an angel, Chen, an angel. That's the only thing that makes any sense to me! I don't have the words to tell you how I feel, or what this means' – he looked skyward – 'but you didn't just give Aaron back his life, but mine and Gemma's too. Thank you, from the bottom of my heart, forever, thank you...'

'You wanna watch the rest of the match, Dad?' *Dad... Dad...* oh to be called by that name! 'I've paused it.' Aaron called out.

'Coming, son.' Mikey took a deep breath and walked back into the house where his boy was waiting.

Epilogue - Chen

I hear them and feel them, you know, every word of thanks, every silent kiss, every quiet prayer of gratitude.

I remember Benjamin Stokes-Rattigan asking, *so what's in it for you?*

Truthfully?

It's these messages of thanks – that's what's in it for me.

To know I chose wisely, made a difference.

Thank you for journeying with me, for letting me give you a little insight, a glimpse into the world of time regifted. And yes, it's sad, but also wonderful that those summoned never know that this is their extra time.

Fifteen minutes, give or take.

The impossible made possible!

I see how most people find life hard, sweating the small stuff, not realising that *everything* is the small stuff! Because sooner than you'd like to think, you'll be forgotten, your possessions discarded, your home someone else's, and all that will remain is the lingering essence of you for as long as someone dare speak your name. But even to them, the details of your face, the exact pitch of your voice, the shape of you, all of it will fade until it's gone altogether.

And as for time – when you wake and look at the person laying with their head on the pillow next to you – ask yourself this, 'How do you know where in time this falls? Is it now, *right now,* the present, or could it be in golden moments between time; their time or yours? A moment when the person you are looking at has called it back, chasing one final glimpse of you.

The answer is, you don't know, how could you? But if I can offer you some wise counsel, I would say this: treat that moment as if it could be either, and you won't go far wrong.

Don't fear death.

Don't be afraid.

It isn't always the neat goodbye you think it is, because in the future at one hour to midnight, someone might choose you.

I expect you're wondering what happened to the people you have read about. Well, it would go against every code of ethics and each agreed and heavily protected working practice for me to have taken a peep into the future and checked up on them.

I can't help anyone to travel forward, no one can do that, but peep at what lies ahead? It's possible.

Oh, what the hell, we've come this far, here's what I saw:

Violet Katherine Drummond passed away aged ninety-nine, surrounded by her family. Her granddaughter, Natalie, swears her nan reached past her and said, 'Here he is! Hello, my love!' just before she died. She believes it was Harry come to take her home.

I think she might be right.

Lewis Mark Noble never remarried. But he did learn how to make a meal out of nothing, mastered laundry, and somehow managed to keep track of all the cards that needed sending to his family. He figured out how to make the house feel cosy and even grew plants. He remembered most of the names of their neighbours, and could get stains out of the rug, even duck shit. He made a fair attempt at making Christmas special, and he learned to live a good life. A life steeped in grief, but a good life, nevertheless.

He ate dinner with his mother-in-law every single Sunday until she passed away.

Sadly, he never mastered how to plump a cushion.

Ruby Jade Brown went on to do great, great things! She gained her doctorate and became a celebrated activist, advocating for young women who found themselves in need of guidance and support when pregnant.

She married Leyton and went on to have three daughters, seven grandchildren (four girls, three boys!) and two great-grandchildren (two girls!).

She lived a full life, a life that made a difference. She kept her promise and did it for her – and Sahara, who never got the chance.

Verity Louise Clarke married her Patrick and lived happily. The two returned to the Highlands with their young twins and set up their own rural practice. Sadly, there was still a need for an infernal computer.

Her father, Dr Rodney, passed away only weeks after the high-profile court case that saw Jon Morton sentenced to life imprisonment for the murder of Grace Rosemary Clarke.

During the trial – a new photograph of Gracie was circulated, one showing her laughing, her inner light shining for all to see.

Oh, and Janice finally quit smoking.

Benjamin Stokes-Rattigan never stopped travelling. He grew his hair, wore sandals, and answered only to 'Ben,' as he hopped from country to country, working in bars, and doing manual labour when he ran out of beer money.

He lost his fancy watch, but, by the time he realised it was missing, had no idea where it had gone. Ah, yes, that fancy watch, a decade old at least, owned by a man who knew what he wanted out of life and how to live it.

A man who found peace by stepping out of his father's shadow, a dark, cold place where his brother, Marcus, lived out his days.

Ben's inheritance sat in a bank account for decades, until he finally, having found his sealegs, dipped into it and bought a sailboat, which he and his partner, Matthew, sailed into the sunset. He did so without a hint of sea sickness.

Occasionally, he sent postcards to his stepmother, Allegra, and of course his lovely, lovely mother whom he always adored and who adored him in return.

Mikey Charles Frewin became a rare example of a contented man. Someone who took joy in the smallest things and woke each day thankful to be alive. He and Gemma were married for nearly seven decades and, in their latter years, doted on their grandson, Mikey Jnr, who became a footballer!

The fact he played for the Blues and not the Reds was rarely mentioned.

Aaron married a woman called Wendy Salmon – which always made his dad laugh, knowing he and Gemma had given their adored son good advice when they told him there were plenty more fish in the sea!

Wendy was a remarkable woman, a mental health nurse who knew enough about depression to help Aaron through the dark days, which were infrequent but still there, lurking like a trap door.

Mikey, over the years, managed to convince himself that losing Aaron had been a nightmare, the very worst kind of dream. It was how he made sense of it.

At least that's what he said, and yet still I heard him, every night before he went to sleep, whispering, 'Thank you, Chen, thank you.'

Goodness, will you look at the clock!

I really must be going.

I have people to visit.

Until the next time…

Chen

About The Author - Amanda Prowse

My name is Amanda Prowse, now nearly sixty, I started writing in my mid-forties. I divide my time between London where I live by the river and our farm in the West Country.

My stories sometimes punch you in the gut with their realism but also leave you with a glimmer of hope – and the feeling that you are not alone. Tales that will make you ugly cry and laugh out loud – sometimes on the same page!

I've sold millions of books, translated into dozens of languages all around the world. Described by the Daily Mail as 'The queen of family drama.' I'm a huge supporter of libraries and am a proud ambassador for The Reading Agency.

My ambition is to create stories that keep people from turning the bedside lamp off at night, great characters that ensure you take every step with them and tales that fill your head so you can't possibly read another book until the memory fades...

Connect with me:

Friend me on Facebook: www.facebook.com/AmandaProwseAuthor

Tag me on Instagram: www.instagram.com/MrsAmandaProwse

Visit my Amazon Author Page: Amanda Prowse Author

Check out my website: www.amandaprowse.com

See my Goodreads page: Goodreads – Amanda Prowse

www.ingramcontent.com/pod-product-compliance
Lightning Source LLC
LaVergne TN
LVHW051004080826
845145LV00009B/2445

* 9 7 8 1 9 1 5 4 0 0 0 9 3 *